The Shift

A Paranormal Women's Fiction Novel

Mia Fliers

Copyright © 2020 Mia Fliers
Cover Art & Design © 2019 Jen Valena

ISBN: 978-1-7347506-1-4

For Jen.
It wouldn't have happened without her.

CHAPTER 1

Brit felt uneasy, restless, not sure where to put her energy. As she moved toward the pantry to retrieve the last of her few coffee beans, the earth seemed to shift beneath her feet. She stood very still. Another aftershock? By now, she certainly should be used to these underground rumblings. As the floor settled once more, she breathed again and reached into the pantry for the coffee beans.

She released her tension, but still sighed in frustration. There were plenty of chores that needed her attention, but she lacked any motivation to begin vacuuming or even dusting her large dome house.

Built by her absent husband, Noah, three years ago, she had at last begun to appreciate this home, especially after the Big One had demolished almost everything around them. How would she have survived in their home in Los Angeles? What if she hadn't been here in the North Valley?

She wondered how Gemma had fared. The image of Gem seemed imprinted on her mind these days.

She had been so close to her. What had driven them apart? Well, she knew it was her husband, Noah. He reacted to Gem's—what he called—obsessive—drive, whether it was politics or religion. Maybe she was. But Brit could certainly use her drive right now!

Brit put the kettle on the stove and began grinding the last of these precious coffee beans when the front door gong sounded.

Startled, Brit stopped her preparations and drew her robe close around her as she headed toward the door. Wondering who it could possibly be, she peered through the door's small window. Gemma!

Opening the door, she exclaimed, "Gemma! You're here!"

"Didn't you expect me?"

"Of course not! How could I? Come in, please."

Gemma swept in, tall, regal, her dark auburn hair piled high. As she entered, she removed her cloak with a flourish.

Brit took it from her, shaking her head and smiling at Gem's usual theatricality. She led her to the kitchen area. "I was just making coffee. I'm so happy to share." She put out two mugs and her last packet of sugar, remembering how Gem loved sugar in her coffee. She wondered how long they would have the luxury of sugar.

Over the freshly ground beans, she poured hot water, which released their rich, dark fragrance as it dripped into the glass pot. "Please sit. Tell me everything."

Gemma sat, observing that Brit was still in her robe, but said nothing.

Brit stared back. "What is it, Gem? Why are you here?"

"That's what you are to tell me. You called me here. Why?"

Brit studied her as she poured the coffee. She brought their mugs to the table.

She focused on Gem's tightly controlled facial expression. Neither the commanding tone in Gemma's voice nor her upright bearing could hide her fatigue.

Brit took her time before speaking. "The phone lines and cell towers are still down. How could I call you?"

"You know very well," Gem said as she stirred the sugar into her coffee. "You have to acknowledge it. The Shift has happened."

Brit bit back her initial denial as she sat, then

observed how tightly she was clasping her hands in her lap. She straightened up in her chair, "For days I've been seeing you very clearly in my mind. But I did not send you any message."

Gem huffed.

Brit continued, "I am glad you came. But I have no plan, no agenda—except to find a way to bring us—all of us—together again." She looked at the smirk on Gem's face. "Yes, I admit it. I do miss everyone."

"Sounds like a message to me," Gem said.

"You call it The Shift. I'm not ready to go that far."

Gem broke in, "Oh really, Brit. How else could I know I had to come, especially after our last conversation?"

"Earthquake or not, I'm so sorry we parted that way."

"Not important."

Brit took a big breath, ready to respond sharply but decided not to, at least not out loud. Not important. *Of course, it was important!* Instead, she said, "When we moved up here permanently, I thought I might never see you again." Brit sighed. "Everyone is scattered."

"But not lost," Gemma said. "Risa is still at her ranch as far as I know. Lilla was heading North. Misha stayed in LA until all hell broke loose. And then I don't know what happened to her."

"And you?"

"I've got a small place at the far end of this valley. I walked here in a day."

"You walked?"

"How else?"

Brit smiled, "You are determined; I'll give you that— and incredibly strong. I really have missed you."

They both sipped the fragrant coffee, relishing the unaccustomed taste.

After a comfortable silence, Gem asked, "How is Noah?"

"He's gone." Brit sighed deeply, not looking at Gemma, but then said, "It's been weeks since he left for Los Angeles."

"Why there?"

"To see if he could gather any of the others. I know how strange that sounds given his anger at the Elders. But he always cared about the people."

Gem nodded.

Brit declared, "All we hear are rumors or crazy speculations about the widespread Upheavals. Did the 'Big One' flatten the city? Is anything left? How many survivors? What about fires?" She took a final swallow, savoring the delicious taste. "People have seen smoke."

Brit took their empty mugs to the sink. "I really

wanted to know whether our house is still standing. I doubt that anything is left." She sat again. "Noah is supposed to come back... I wish The Shift did happen —to *all* of us. No communication drives me crazy."

"Have you tried?"

Brit inhaled sharply. "Not consciously, no."

Gemma leaned toward Brit. "There are two of us now. We could focus our energy together." She looked at Brit's skeptical expression. "Come on! We'll make it a test. See who shows up." Her rare smile softened Brit into a half-hearted nod.

Gemma rose to give Brit a hug, but they were interrupted by the gong, resounding once again throughout the dome house.

Brit quickly stood, wishing she had dressed that morning. She moved to the door. *Who could that be?* Not sure whether to be fearful or excited, she looked through the window and quickly opened the door.

"Misha?" Brit couldn't believe this waif in tattered clothes could be her sweet Misha.

"It's all right that I came?" Misha asked.

"Oh, my dear. Come in. Come in."

She gave Misha a welcoming hug and felt how thin she had become. "Gemma is here too."

Gemma opened her arms to Misha while giving Brit a

'now-do-you-believe' look.

Brit ignored Gemma as she took in Misha's bedraggled appearance. *What had happened to her?*

"How far have you come?" Brit asked as she took her worn jacket.

"I had no way to know how far away you were."

Brit glanced at Gem with a questioning look, then turned back to Misha. "We'll talk about everything later. You are shivering. What you need is a hot bath! I'll find something clean for you to wear." She started ushering her to the bathroom, but stopped as she thought to ask, "Are you hungry? Thirsty?"

"A glass of water, please."

"Of course! Gem, would you get that, please?"

"Coming right up."

Brit kept a constant patter going as she led Misha to the bathroom and began running water into the tub.

"You get in the tub. I'll be right back."

Misha had sunk into the warm water when Brit returned with a glass of water. Misha took it gratefully and drank all of it down. Brit pulled down from the cabinet scented soap and shampoo.

"Thank you so much."

"Towels are here. I'll put clothes on the bed. Is there anything else you need?"

Misha shook her head. Then with a gentle smile, she said, "I would like to just sit in the water for a bit."

"Take as much time as you need," assured Brit. "I will be in the next room—dressing."

When Brit came back into the kitchen, Gem offered, "What you need is a calming cup of herbal tea." She put the kettle on to boil.

Brit pulled out a chair as she tried to put together the puzzle of Misha's arrival. She looked at Gem. "What do you make of all that?"

Gemma smiled enigmatically and busied herself making tea.

The women were quiet, waiting for the kettle to boil, both puzzling over Misha's arrival.

Misha came into the kitchen, still drying her hair. As she approached the two women, she said, "I was so relieved when I saw your dome. You made it through the Upheavals." She sat in the chair that Gem pulled from the table for her. "Noah knew it all along."

Misha's five-foot two-inch frame looked tiny in the large garments that Brit had found for her. Her long, silvery-blond hair, still damp, clung to her shoulders.

Misha looked at Gem. "When did you get the

message?"

Gemma looked at Brit and then at Misha. "What message did you get?"

Misha looked puzzled.."To come to the Gathering, of course. Didn't you?"

"Yes. I did. Exactly," said Gemma.

"I've never Heard so clearly before. I was quite excited." She looked at Brit, "I wasn't sure anyone else Heard in the same way."

Gem asked, "Did you say you've Heard?" Her shoulders lifted in question.

Misha hesitated, then pushed back her hair. "Yes, but not so clearly. I've tried to share," she glanced at Gemma, "but not many wanted to listen. It should be different now, don't you think?"

Brit listened, still wanting to question what was becoming obvious. *If the Shift has happened, then why can't I Hear Noah?*

"How widespread—" Brit began to ask, but was cut off by the gong once again.

Brit hurried to answer the door. A quick look verified her anticipation. "Risa!" she said, watching her dismount. Still up on her 'high' horse, she stifled a laugh as she went to greet her and then saw Lilla standing beside the door.

"Hola! You survived," Lilla announced, barging in without an invitation to give Brit her usual air kiss. "Good. I wondered whether the dome would withstand the Upheavals. Where is Noah? I'd like to congratulate him," she said, shaking her raven-black curls.

"Not here right now," Brit answered as she gathered Lilla's heavy poncho. "Did you come together?"

"Not hardly!" Risa said with a hint of sarcasm. "We met at the fork. We discovered that both of us were *hopefully* heading toward the dome."

"Gem and Misha are in the kitchen area," Brit said, indicating the direction.

Lilla stepped around Risa and headed to the kitchen.

Risa stayed with Brit, who was hanging up Lilla's poncho.

"I want to know; has it happened?" demanded Risa.

Brit turned to her and asked, "If not, why did you come?"

"To see if I imagined the whole thing," Risa said.

"Maybe you did." Brit smiled at her as she took Risa's leathers. "Please. Go on in; join the others."

Brit wished she had more refreshments to offer. Replenishing supplies had become very difficult. Here in the North Valley, they were dependent on supplies being delivered from the city. Transportation was at a standstill since there were no trucks delivering gasoline.

Noah had stocked their emergency stores well. But still...

Brit had put herself on a limited diet when he left. She was afraid of running out and being unable to buy more.

She wished her husband, Noah, was here now. Maybe he wouldn't know what to do any more than she did. But just to be able to talk together... assuming he was talking to her at all.

Laughter from the kitchen, and Lilla's voice ringing out "Hola!" caught her attention.

Maybe all of us together can find a way—to what? Brit tried to shake off her gloomy thoughts as she joined the others.

In the cupboard, Brit had found more tea, and the chattering died down as each enjoyed the treat. Misha was curled up in the swivel chair. Risa was attempting to pin up her long, blond braids as Gemma lounged on the sofa. Lilla, twisting her shiny black ringlets, sat cross-legged on the rug, leaning against the kitchen island.

Brit sat in her usual captain's chair, grateful for the camaraderie. She hoped it would last. She wished she had taken the time this morning to do more than put a brush to her honey-blond hair.

It had been a long time since they had actually enjoyed being together. Why had they come together? How long would this peaceful respite last, she wondered?

After taking them on a tour of the dome house, Brit directed them to sleeping quarters in the adjacent dome. *Noah's foresight again.*

She took Gemma aside, asking her to stay behind. They went into Brit's sitting/sleeping area, which Brit was able to close off from the rest of the dome.

"I really need to talk with you," Brit said.

"That's fine." Gemma took one of the comfy armchairs across from Brit.

"Do we need to clear the air?" asked Brit.

"We're fine," assured Gemma. "I'm happy we can work together again, or at least it feels that way."

"We have to!" Brit said. "I've been so alone here since Noah left. I had no idea that all of us had come

North. Do you think anyone else may be coming?"

"We should probably ask Misha," Gem smiled. "She's obviously the most tuned in to The Shift."

"You are convinced that what we are experiencing is The Shift? Not just some anomaly?"

Gemma stretched the kinks out of her shoulders. "I don't care what we call it. Whatever it is, we need to harness it. Investigate and experiment."

Gemma watched Brit wringing her hands. "What are you worrying about?"

"Food, shelter, purpose."

"Stop the moaning. Those are our problems to solve, not just yours."

Brit gave a short laugh and quickly wiped the threatening tears away. "OK," she sniffed. "I really have missed you."

Gemma sat still for a moment, and then asked, "Why did you and Noah leave?"

"Noah left before I did. I felt I had to stay in LA for the sake of the Gatherers." Brit put her head in her hands. "I couldn't—I don't know what 'I couldn't.' Finally, I knew I had to stop pretending that everything was fine. I had to leave The Gathering.

"Noah had become disillusioned with the Elders long before I was ready to give up. He knew I had to reach that point by myself. I was so engrossed with trying to hold everything together, I didn't realize how distant he had become. Basically, we had stopped talking altogether.

"He had never told me about this land, which he had inherited from his parents before we met. But with no discussion of any kind, he commissioned a man from Colorado, who had built dome houses, to build this." She motioned around her. "I was so angry he hadn't told me I was fit to be tied."

Gem asked, "Why did he keep it a secret from you—from everyone—or almost everyone?"

"He had left for good, but he didn't want me to know that.

"And then I crashed. Thank heaven he wanted to help pick up the pieces." Brit breathed a watery sigh. "By the time I was finished with The Gathering, this place was ready. He had even stocked it with emergency supplies—water, food, everything.

"He welcomed me here to heal."

Gem asked, "What did the Elders say?"

"I've no idea. I left without a word. Not too brave, I guess. But escape was the only thought in my mind. Noah was way ahead of me."

"So, you don't know what happened to the Gathering

after you left?"

"No. Once up here in the North Valley, we shut off all communication, just before the Big One hit. The Upheavals finished it for us. When I thought about the Gathering at all, I guessed you or Risa, or even Lilla, would take on the leadership."

Gem shook her head. "After the Mega-quake, the Gathering fell apart. People just started leaving." She snorted. "Even some of the Elders. Most of them no longer even tried to fake answers for all the questions bombarding them.

"As far as I knew, Risa was at her horse ranch. She never really committed to leaving it, as you know." Gem barked a sharp laugh. "The Elders weren't too happy about that."

Brit nodded, "Yes, I knew that. I was assigned the task of persuading her to sign her ranch over to them. Thank goodness she is so stubborn."

Gem looked surprised. "I didn't know they would go that far."

Brit looked up at Gemma, nodded, and with a heavy sigh, said, "It was more than I could stomach."

Neither said anything for a time.

Then Brit asked, "What about Lilla?"

Gemma sat up straighter in her chair. "Lilla told no

one where she was headed. 'Just North' is all she said. I guess this is as far North as she got. Her two boys apparently are still with her. She mentioned they were home."

"What about her husband?" Brit asked.

"He left before anyone else thought of leaving. He was just waiting for an excuse."

"Poor Lilla."

"Hardly," said Gem. "That marriage was doomed from the start."

Brit winced at Gem's harsh assessment. "And Misha?"

Gem gave Brit a quizzical look. "She knew, somehow. Maybe she Heard like she said. The Upheavals didn't take her by surprise. The week before the Big One hit LA, she packed her stuff and left. She tried to tell me, but I brushed her off."

"Is that when you left?"

Gemma made a face, "Oh No! I had to have my home collapse around my feet before I got the message that it was time to leave."

"How awful," Brit said. "But you had a place here, in the North Valley?"

"My mom had a summer cabin she left to me. It took some time, but I found it—rustic but intact—and I've been there since."

"About Misha; you are saying Misha Knew before the Upheavals began?"

"Yes."

"That just confuses the issue, doesn't it?" said Brit.

"The issue isn't whether The Shift has happened. It has. We are here; we were called here. Misha is a separate case. We've always known she was a sensitive. Somehow she Knows things—"

Brit interjected, "She says she Hears—what? Voices?"

Gem said, "I think we need to ask her. In fact, I think she needs to help us learn to Hear our own inner voices."

After a big yawn, she continued, "We know at least that the five of us are on the same channel. We have to make use of that." Another yawn overtook her.

Brit got up, extending a hand to Gemma, "Come on, let's get you to a bed. We will all think more clearly in the morning."

CHAPTER 2

Once Gemma was settled for the night, Brit's restlessness sent her to the kitchen for another cup of tea. She was pensive. There were too many unanswered questions she didn't want to address.

Before the Upheavals, she had begun to ask difficult questions, ones that the Elders were unable, or unwilling to answer or even discuss. Her relationship with the Elders had become increasingly awkward.

When she tried to share her experiences with them, their perception seemed stuck, never changing or evolving. She tried to retreat into her own meditation practice, but people began seeking her out, wanting solutions to their own personal issues. They wanted answers from her. She had none to give.

Brit knew she had no business giving solutions to their problems, and yet they did their best to pull answers from her. At times she seemed to 'channel'—or whatever it was—answers they wanted, however unwilling she was to give them.

She had always debunked anything seemingly paranormal until it started happening to her. At first, it was just a sense of Knowing. When her meditation started to bring forth visions, she stopped meditating, which left her feeling empty and lost.

She resisted sharing what was happening, fearing that she would be considered crazy or even possessed. When she confessed to the Elders, they clung to their mantra: Peace within is peace. Seek the Elder, not each other. Your answer is in the divine source, held only by the Elders, not in your deluded mind.

As more and more gatherers were Hearing—and Listening—to their own inner voice, they were told to ignore them and consider them demons!

Brit shook her head as she remembered her disbelief when hearing reports of such superstitious nonsense. Noah just smiled enigmatically when she tried to share with him. No help there!

She returned her cup to the sink, rinsing it as she tried to place exactly when everything had changed. Almost three years ago, she thought. The early rumblings, mini-quakes started about then.

It was at the same time people started talking about a Shift, not just of the earth, but in people as well. The New Agers were proclaiming their unique abilities to predict events and to Know what others were thinking.

Brit wanted to dismiss their claims as nonsense, but she couldn't ignore her own experiences of Knowing and even channeling. She struggled with the temptation to just 'go with it.' She became convinced that no one wanted to hear her concerns.

The Elders talked about the divine muse. That scared her even more. She had no inclination to seek or to become anyone's guru. It went against her belief that each of us is an embodiment of the divine, and therefore each of us should empower ourselves and others.

She sighed. If even that idea was real.

She retreated once again to her bedroom. She certainly wasn't 'channeling' any answers tonight. She needed sleep. Tomorrow was looming.

* * *

As tired as Risa was, she found it hard to fall asleep. She missed her own safe haven with its comforting smells of horses and other animals that roamed her ranch. She loved the sweet scent of springtime grasses, which had just started to grow when she left.

She tossed and turned to find a comfortable spot on the cot. How lucky she had been to be at her ranch when the 'Big One' hit. As refugees started showing up, she put the capable and willing ones to work in exchange for food and shelter. She learned to conserve.

She was so glad she got the fencing put up. The urgency she felt to protect her place with the high fence turned out to be very wise. Most strangers bypassed what appeared from a distance to be a burned-out ranch. Others took a chance, hoping for handouts or even work. Risa did her best to find meaningful tasks. The few who came she assigned to fence in a grassy meadow for her horses. It wasn't readily seen by people heading North.

She turned onto her back, her thoughts not letting her sleep yet. Two years, maybe more before the Upheavals began—a good description. She thought of all the changes since the mini-quakes and so-called aftershocks that seemed to never stop. Weird how one could get used to the earth constantly moving under your feet.

The urgent impulse 'to leave and find the others' took

her by surprise. She had left LA, feeling very done with the growing superstitious nonsense being spouted by the Gatherers and the Elders.

Why now this impulse to seek out Brit? Noah, she could talk to. But then Brit had become so unreachable, distant, even severe. Of course, Brit's and the Elders' pompous attitude was a big reason why Risa had left the Gathering! Her reality was found in and on the earth, not in some Super Divine. She had only intuited she had to find the other women again.

Risa felt confident that Carmela could take charge of the women who worked in the house and cooked for the hired hands on the ranch. She could trust her to take care of the animals as well. Carlos, her foreman, assured her that he would protect the ranch. Risa had mounted supplies onto her palomino and headed—for where?

She only intuited she had to find them. Would they still be in Los Angeles? Or what was left of it. Well, she would start her search there.

Risa got supplies mounted on her palomino and tried to head South.

She chuckled as she snuggled into the covers, remembering how her stubborn horse had refused to go in any direction except North! No matter how she reined him toward the South, he wouldn't move unless they headed North. Her frustration mounted until an image of Brit had filled her mind, and then a picture of a dome. Noah's dome! Somehow, she knew he had finally done it. Brit and Noah must be there.

Feeling an urgency to find them, she gave in to Sunshine. She would look for the dome. Her horse, Sunshine, already seemed to know the way.

With that final memory of heading North, she nodded off.

* * *

Misha waited until she sensed that everyone was asleep. She got up quietly and went out the front door. She needed the scents and sounds of the night and the soft soughing of the nearby pine forest. The stars glowed like giant crystals throughout the sky. She could breathe again.

It wasn't going to be easy to unite the five women. Risa had never listened to her. Even Brit seemed wishy-washy about The Shift, but at least she was learning to honor her own inner voices. Misha knew Brit Heard. She wasn't sure Brit knew.

Gemma would make sure everyone's practical needs were met, even if she didn't acknowledge to the others that she was being guided.

Lilla was the renegade. Time would tell. She would go along with a plan if it suited her own desires. Misha took in a deep breath, relishing the piney scent. She wondered if Noah was one of Lilla's desires. Maybe it was a good thing he wasn't here, although Misha was disappointed not to find him here—and in charge at last!

She went inside again, hoping to be able to sleep. Maybe tomorrow she could set up a private space for herself nearby, but out in the open air. If she could dream, maybe her plan would take shape.

* * *

Lilla was the first one awake in the morning. She craved that first cup of coffee. Good thing she brought her own supply. She supposed she would have to share it with the others. She sighed in resignation.

A new thought came to her. If she shared, it would get everyone on her side, and maybe a way to heal the rift between Brit and her.

Did Brit know about her and Noah? She had thought Brit too naïve—or too self-absorbed—to pick up on that vibe. It had definitely been a mistake and best forgotten. Actually, lucky he was not here—but she wondered where he was.

She got the coffee brewing, expecting the aroma to awaken the others. She smirked to herself, fully aware of her own self-absorption and pleased she could present herself in a beneficial light.

Lilla hummed as the coffee brewed. She would even share a packet of her sugar. She smiled. That would impress Gemma.

She heard the women stirring. *What would today bring?*

* * *

Brit came into the kitchen, smelling the coffee. Everyone had made use of their own nutrition packs. But who? She saw Lilla's Cheshire-cat smile and knew at once where the coffee came from—and why.

"Lilla—this is so generous of you, and believe me, so appreciated!" Brit said as she took her first sip. "Sorry, I overslept. I guess I was really tired," she said. "Have you found everything you need?"

Risa spoke up, "I found the greenhouse dome! What a luxury to have fresh greens. That must have been Noah's inspiration." She lifted one eyebrow. "Unless, of course, you've developed a green thumb."

"Yes, I think he was the one inspired," said Brit.

Lilla piped up, "How did he figure out refrigeration without electricity?"

A pretty perceptive question, coming from Lilla, thought Brit.

"A root cellar takes care of most of our needs. Plant foods have become our staple diet. Once in awhile he would hunt, but we needed to prepare and cook it right away. When there is winter snow, we can use it to keep the meat a little longer. And of course, solar panels help."

Gemma broke in, "We have more important things to discuss than Noah's inventions."

Brit smiled in appreciation for the change in subject away from Noah.

Brit relished having company. In the past, even when they bickered, they had been her family. *And I just left them.*

She gathered up the breakfast things and began washing dishes as she thought about how they had been before they were torn apart by rancor and disillusion. Old issues unresolved surfaced for each one. Idealistic ideas of unity in diversity seemed impossible. Even their toning was more chaotic than musical. Their squabbles were petty, even childish.

She started drying and returning the dishes and mugs to the cupboard when a realization stopped her: *Each one of us left The Gathering. Yet here they are. Why did they come? What do they expect? What do they want from me?* She turned to face them.

"As much as I'm enjoying this reunion," Brit said, "I would like to know why each of you came?"

No one spoke.

"I know, you Heard or Felt or Knew—" She waited. "OK, you are here. But why?"

Lilla spoke up first. "As difficult as I found it to support you, I did respect your dedication—to each of us. It was no coincidence that people started leaving when you left. The Gathering fell apart."

Misha added, "Some blamed you. They felt you abandoned them. Others left, just for their own reasons. The rest left after the Big One hit."

"Lilla's right, you know," said Risa. "You were the

glue holding us together. I never would have admitted that then, but it was true. And I didn't think about finding you, I just had to."

"Each of us needs the others," said Gemma. "I know you aren't going to save us from all the chaos or the Upheavals. But maybe together—"

Misha was beaming. Her plan could work. "Ladies, there is a plan—it's not perfect, but a beginning…"

Brit cut in, "Beginning of what?"

Misha continued, "We need to leave here—together—after we have engaged the Circle once more—to guide us."

Lilla's eyes rolled, while Risa just stared at Misha. Gemma, however, appeared to find the idea of re-energizing the Circle intriguing. She saw comprehension on Brit's face.

"You are talking about reactivating The Gathering," Brit said.

"Not the same. Just us. Committed to each other, accessing all-that-is—"

Gemma cut her off. "We become the new Elders? Ha! No, thank you!"

Misha wasn't about to give up. "What I have 'Heard'—no Elders. Only be available guides to those who seek us." She looked around at their uncomprehending expressions. "We must strengthen our bonds. The Circle works—we all know this."

Lilla shrugged and said, "Look, I tried before; I did exactly what I was told: I visualized, saw exactly what I wanted. OK, needed—and knew exactly how to get it—and zilch."

Shaking her head, Misha explained, "Not that way. Opening to each other and then to all others without an agenda, just the intent to bring Love—"

"It sounds lovely," Brit said as she put her hand on Misha's shoulder, "but exactly how do we do that?"

Misha smiled at each one and said, "The Circle. First, we activate our own energy and then intertwine our energies. I've 'Heard' how to do this."

There was silence as they tried to wrap their minds around what Misha proposed.

"We *could* try the Circle again," Gemma suggested.

Lilla piped up, "I like the toning."

Risa commented, "In harmony this time please." Before Lilla could take offense, she saw that Risa was smiling at her.

Brit said, "All right, but I don't want to lead—"

"No one leads," said Gemma.

"Right!" said Misha. "At first, we each take a turn leading. Then, as we learn to support one another, there will be no need for a leader."

"So, we learn from each other, sharing the role equally," Gemma offered.

"Exactly!" said Misha. "We'll learn as we try." In a more serious tone, she said, "We must accept that this is not for ourselves, but for the good of all." Looking at their faces, she reassured them, "That includes us, of course!"

"It sounds a little woo-woo to me." Risa shot a quick glance at Lilla. "I liked the toning too."

Brit chimed in, "I think we all loved The Circle. There is no reason not to try to reactivate *that* practice. I'm willing to follow Misha's lead... until I can't."

Brit continued, "We also have practical matters to address. I see you have each brought your own nutrition packs. I am very grateful for that. I know you have seen the small greenhouse dome. My supplies, however, are limited, and with the five of us..."

She was stopped by Gemma. "What can we do?"

Brit sighed with relief. "Would you help me inventory the supplies we have on hand, including what each of you brought?"

Gemma quickly agreed and spoke to the others. "We need a plan." Looking at their confused expressions, she went on. "Get together and brainstorm, get ideas;

defining our intention should be the first priority." She followed behind Brit out the door.

* * *

That night Brit slept fitfully, although she was worn out from all the sorting and noting of what was available and estimating how long all of it would last.

The dream came again. She could see Noah through that glass wall that separated them. He was trying to tell her something. His gestures got bigger and wilder as he tried to make her understand. She pounded on the glass wall, but he couldn't hear it. Finally, he threw up his hands in anger and despair, turned, and left.

She felt a chokehold around her neck as she thrashed in the suffocating bedclothes. She couldn't escape!

She woke, sitting straight up in bed, tears cascading from her eyes. "Breathe," she voiced. "Just breathe." In a couple of minutes, her breath came more easily and finally slowed to a normal rate.

She got herself to her bathroom and splashed cold water on her face. Brit looked in the mirror and asked aloud, "Where is he? Why isn't he back? Will he ever come back?"

CHAPTER 3

"Please, Brit!"

Noah had tried to coax Brit into coming to the North Valley to see the dome for herself.

But just looking at her facial expression told him it was a mistake.

His plea just reignited their ongoing argument. He wanted to get out of Los Angeles while they could. But she insisted that she couldn't 'just leave' the Gatherers in her charge.

Brit was furious that he hadn't discussed all this with her before starting, what she considered, a ridiculously expensive project. Besides, she argued, no one could predict when the so-called Big One would hit.

He was convinced that the earth's rumblings were a prelude to the long-awaited Big One.

After researching, he had become convinced that a

dome house would survive 300 mile per hour winds as well as a Mega-Earthquake. Noah went North alone.

His parents had left him 40 acres of land in the North Valley when they passed. When he was in Colorado going to school, he had become friends with George, a Civil Engineer who specialized in building dome structures. Noah was intrigued and began doing research on his own.

When Noah got in touch with George and offered him an opportunity to build Noah's very special dome house, his friend jumped at the chance.

Noah asked George to build a smaller dome first that he could utilize as a greenhouse as the larger structures were being constructed. Planting and working with the plants as they grew began to fill Noah with the peace he had been seeking.

If only Brit would come—even to visit, he felt that eventually she would come around. In the meantime, he spent much of his time searching for the right tools, the heirloom seeds for his greenhouse as well as for a garden, and a hard-to-find solar generator.

As the dome house neared completion, he knew he

had to go back one last time to LA. First, to try to persuade Brit one final time; Secondly, he was determined to finish his separation from The Gathering, or at least from the Leaders. The Elders be damned.

As angry as Brit felt, she wondered whether she had made a mistake, staying in LA when Noah went North. If she and Noah were to stay together, the compromise most likely would have to come from her.

What if she spent a little time away to check out Noah's project? Gemma could take over for her while she was away. Risa and Lilla would support her.

Telling the Elders her plan wasn't pleasant, but she made a case that she would convince Noah to come back to The Gathering. She had little hope for success, but to soothe her conscience, she would try.

Brit had her own doubts about the growing rigidity dictated by the Elders. She had rationalized until she couldn't anymore. Nor did the increasing mini-quakes support her skepticism about Noah's insistence that they had to leave Los Angeles.

Her own meditation deepened significantly as she confronted her doubts and fears. It was clear to her that transparency among The Gathering, an ideal she sought, was going in the opposite direction. Secret cliques, promoted by the Elders, had developed along with petty jealousies and backstabbing—even among her closest friends. She couldn't imagine what they would do if the Big One did happen.

This beautiful community she had devoted her life to —what happened? Even the women she depended upon were increasingly distant. She didn't know how to reach them. All communication was superficial at best.

Maybe getting away for a little while, would help. Noah had urged her to come, just for a visit. At least it would show Noah she was attempting to honor their relationship. And if it couldn't be salvaged? At least she had tried.

Knocking interrupted Brit's reverie.

As Misha rapped on Brit's door, she called, "May I come in?"

"Of course," Brit said as she ushered her into the sitting area. "What do you need?" She assumed that was the issue.

Misha smiled at her. She took one of the chairs and looked intently at Brit. "We need to make our Circle tonight. It's—urgent."

Brit asked, "Have you talked to the others? Do they want this?"

Misha rose. "It's what must be done."

Her intense manner surprised Brit. This wasn't the Misha she was used to. "What makes you so sure?"

Misha didn't answer Brit's question. Instead, she asked, "Do you have a preference as to where it takes place? The only condition is that it be outside, sometime this evening as it turns to night."

"It's fine with me, but the others may not—"

Misha put her hand on Brit's arm. "That should no longer concern you. They are here. They are the ones who came. It's my concern now."

She smiled reassuringly at Brit and left, quietly shutting the door behind her.

CHAPTER 4

At sunset, the women gathered. Misha had found an appropriate grassy area and then pushed and pulled five stones into a circle, one for each woman. At Misha's instruction, each found a place by a stone within the circle. They extended their arms to touch the hands of the women on either side of her.

Misha began the hum. Each joined, focusing on the initial pitch before finding their own that harmonized with the others.

It was discordant at first. But these women at one time had been accomplished practitioners. Their toning began to take on a resonance that intertwined with their individual energies into one.

They each felt the One.

Misha guided the ebb and flow of sound and then let it fade and cease. The remaining silence held the sound.

Their bodies released the vibrations and then became still. Their breathing had become synchronized.

Misha sank down to sit on her stone; the others followed.

She then spoke: "Has the intent been intuited?"

As one, they replied, "We are the Circle of Intent."

No more was said. Their meditation filled the night.

After a time, Misha rose; the others followed her lead.

As the women returned to the dome, Misha turned away and headed toward the pine forest. It was calling her. Once there, she took in deep breaths of the pungent night smells. The night creatures' sounds filled her ears as they bedded down for the night, while others awoke ready to hunt.

She called out to whatever was there, "I've faced my demons!" She listened for reverberating echoes or a response. Fears and doubts were gone, as were self-pity and feelings of helplessness.

The tension she had been holding melted away. She had been so afraid! What if the women couldn't Hear her? But they did! And the Circle embraced them.

After a time, she rose and brushed away the pine needles that had stuck to her clothing when she sat. She felt the energy rising from the earth, coursing through her body, supporting her as she walked with purpose and strength to rejoin her sisters in the dome.

* * *

Brit put the kettle on to make tea. No one spoke. Each was involved with her own thoughts. They were together, but separate.

Brit poured the tea, then sat with the others around the kitchen table.

Risa broke the silence. "What now?"

Misha answered her, "We do it again."

Lilla spoke up, "What's the point?"

"We've only begun our training. The Circle of Intent is so much more than we have ever experienced." Misha paused, took a breath, and looked first at Lilla as she reluctantly tried to explain, "Back in the beginning of The Gathering we thought all we had to do was hum, visualize, feel good, and manifest. We thought that was all there was to the Circle. Those were just baby steps. There is so much more."

Brit was astonished by Misha. Where was the little mouse she had cherished? "Are you saying that The Shift has given you some kind of special sight or knowing?"

"Not exactly." Misha gave Brit an appreciative smile. "I experienced the beginnings of The Shift before the Upheavals began. But I didn't recognize what I Heard or Knew as The Shift."

Misha looked around at the others. They were listening to her intently. "Perhaps it is what you are experiencing now." She continued, "Only after the world convulsed in volcanoes and earthquakes did my Knowing increase substantially. I never told anyone, but I realized that what was happening was not only the earth shifting. It was happening in people too."

Gemma asked, "How do we come into the picture… exactly?"

"We've only begun the first steps in healing our Circle of Intent. We must continue to practice together until we are whole. Then we can leave. And we'll know where to go."

There were no more questions.

Misha closed her eyes. She seemed to be listening. When she opened them, she got up from the table and left. They heard the front door open and then close gently.

Risa looked at the other women, "I guess I got my answer."

"I don't know if I can go along with rehashing the Gathering dogma," Lilla announced.

Gemma got up and joined Brit in clearing the table. "There was no dogma in what she said." She turned from the sink. "In fact, I hear the opposite. We need to learn to Listen to the silence until we can Hear and unite our intentions."

Brit chimed in, "I feel a little uneasy, too. But wasn't that the original goal of The Gathering? I know it never happened. The Elders took over, making us believe we weren't worthy; only they could Hear and then tell the rest of us."

Lilla asked, "Isn't that what Misha is doing now?"

"Just the opposite," said Gemma. "I think she is trying to get us to empower ourselves; go beyond what we've done before."

Lilla got up from the table. "I don't know. It just makes my head hurt. I'm going to go for a walk." She left the room.

Brit said, "Good idea. Let's all take a break. See you in the morning."

* * *

Lilla's thoughts were with her boys. She had instructed them to salvage whatever they could from their damaged cabin. They were clever twenty-year-olds. They would find a way to rebuild a shelter from whatever remained from the last quake.

As she walked, she thought about how she had intended to leave The Gathering and LA earlier. The groups had splintered into cliques, and she wanted no part in their petty squabbles. She wanted her whole family to relocate up North. Before that could happen, Jon, her husband, took off, making it clear he wasn't going to return.

He was pretty worthless anyway. For the most part, men are a nuisance, aside from my boys, of course. She chuckled about that to herself. *What should I do? Well, I'm not going to encourage Misha.*

Lilla and her boys had headed North after the 'Big One' hit. She was sure that the LA quake was localized until they met travelers traveling South. They described the devastation they had escaped near Mt. Hood, which was now a very active volcano. Lilla realized how fortunate they were. They arrived at their summer cabin, only intending to rest before going on.

Before Lilla could consider their next step, finding Brit became an obsession—and she left. The boys were upset. They couldn't comprehend her decision. She promised she'd return as soon as she found Brit. She hadn't been able to explain what she didn't understand.

She stopped to catch her breath when she reached the pine forest. When she saw a log stump, she sat and enjoyed the breeze that carried the scent of the pine trees.

She relished the special feeling she experienced that evening in their Circle. It had been years, not since first joining The Gathering, that she had felt that joy! When did it disappear? Could they get it back? Could *they really* make a difference?

She started back to the dome, grateful that the moon had risen, lighting her way. She decided she would stay for now. Just maybe they could develop a force to reach others.

Lilla hadn't hoped for much since the Upheavals had made survival the only priority. Tonight a flicker of hope had ignited. It felt good.

* * *

Risa made herself a cup of ginger tea. She hated being conflicted. Could Misha be on to something?

How would they know? How could re-energizing the Circle make a difference in this devastated world?

She sipped the spicy tea. *The Circle of Intent? What is our intent?*

Risa had intended to go to Los Angeles, not come here! It had seemed important to know if anything of value was left after the gigantic quake. She wanted to help if there were survivors.

She missed Noah's optimism, his assurance that all would be well. They only had to come together, and they could build the beautiful world The Gathering promised. Her anger surfaced as she remembered how those dreams had turned to ashes.

When the Upheavals began, even before the Big Quake, the Elders started micromanaging the Circle. Their fear of losing control was palpable. They put their sycophants in charge. Risa couldn't stand the required spouting of empty platitudes.

Well, she was lucky. She had never left her horse ranch. The Elders tried to intimidate her into signing the ranch over to The Gathering. They made it clear she would never be trusted as a leader unless she released this 'attachment,' as they termed it.

She had never seen herself as one of their so-called leaders, so their ultimatum made it easy to walk away.

Thank heaven I awoke in time from my delusions about The Gathering and those who ran it.

Risa shook her head and then smiled as she remembered how it was only the steady clop, clop of Sunshine's hooves as she rode that soothed her bruised heart.

As she sipped her tea, her thoughts turned to Misha. *Had she been hiding her psychic abilities all this time? Are they real? Oh boy! The Elders would have made mincemeat of her if they knew. That was the issue, wasn't it? No one was to be empowered unless the Elders made it so.*

Risa went to her sleeping space and lay down. She admitted to herself that the toning had filled her up as nothing had in a very long time. OK. For now, she would go along with *that part,* at least.

* * *

Misha returned to the circle of stones and sat down, cross-legged in the middle of the circle. She felt comfortable there, safe even. Before she closed her eyes, she saw Lilla walking away from the dome toward the pines. *Good, the trees will calm her.*

Misha closed her eyes, hoping meditation would quiet her excitement. As she breathed, the count began to regulate her breathing. Breathing in—1, 2, 3—slowly breathing out—4, 5, 6, 7. She visualized her energy begin to move throughout her body, and then expand to include the circle of stones.

A growing realization filled and warmed her. *The Count!* She opened her eyes. This was the next step to bring everyone's energy toward the Intent.

Tomorrow! She got up, feeling far more confident.

* * *

Brit and Gemma left the kitchen together, and in unspoken agreement, retired to the sitting area in Brit's bedroom.

Brit spoke first, "Have you ever seen this, Misha?"

Gemma sat for a moment, thinking. "No. But she wouldn't have dared reveal this self to the Elders. She would have been shunned by decree."

"Yes, of course. That sort of explains the change. But still—"

"Brit," Gemma sounded exasperated, "She is concrete evidence that The Shift is real, and it has happened. Don't you remember how we used to dream and talk about what the world would be like when 'it' happened? It *is* happening. I think Misha is helping each of us awaken to our own abilities and the group's ability to become a force for good."

Brit sighed, then looked at Gem with a smile. "What is very clear to me is that The Shift is not happening equally in each of us."

Gemma wanted to interrupt, but Brit stopped her with a raised hand and continued, "Why can't I reach Noah? Why have only we five come together? What if men haven't changed at all? That would certainly be a problem!"

Gemma urged, "I feel Misha is trying to help us empower ourselves—to reach our full potential—as we used to say." She looked at Brit for confirmation. "Didn't you feel anything in our Circle?"

"Of course I did," snapped Brit. "But I still have questions."

"Misha said we have just begun. Let's continue. See where it goes."

Brit nodded. She admitted to herself that being immersed in the energy created by their toning was thrilling. So, yes, she would go along with Misha's instruction if only to experience the joy again.

She acknowledged Gemma, "Of course, we should continue. I want to explore the possibilities as much as you." She reached for Gemma's hands. It felt so good to have her friend close again.

* * *

The following sunset saw each of them standing erect beside their stones, awaiting Misha's instruction.

She asked them to leave their shoes outside the circle of stones. They complied, wondering what was next.

"Please enter the circle and let your feet meld into the earth."

A minute or two passed. As they sensed the warmth and the feel of the powdery earth under their feet and between their toes, they quieted.

"Sink down and sit on your stone," Misha directed. "Feel the energy of the earth embrace your feet; it moves now to your ankles, your knees, and to your hips.

"Let's begin the count." She initiated the breathing, "Breathe in—1, 2, 3 and exhale 4, 5, 6, 7."

They easily fell into the familiar rhythm of breath in and breath out.

Misha instructed, "Breathe deep, feel the energy move up your spine, now to your third eye, to the brain, and through the top of your head, embracing all others within the Circle."

At the end of one long breath, Misha said, "Now—we. See."

The silence embraced them, energy swirled around them. Tears flowed.

Misha rose to her feet. She raised her arms as if to embrace all of them. "Open your eyes; See anew. Rise toward the sky; let us move into our new world."

She left the Circle. After a moment, they all followed.

CHAPTER 5

Each evening the women gathered as the sun slipped behind the distant mountains. Each one intuited who would initiate the hum or the count. Fewer words of instruction were needed as the week progressed.

When Misha took her turn once more, she said nothing until the ceremony was about to be completed. She lifted her arms to embrace her sisters and asked, "What is the Circle's Intent?

As one, they spoke, "We leave for Los Angeles to find the others."

They re-entered the dome quickly and gathered around the kitchen table. A mutually felt purpose was evident in their postures. Brit started to put the kettle on to boil.

Lilla stopped her. "Forget the tea, Brit. We have to

talk."

There were murmurs of agreement. Brit quickly sat down. *We've agreed to leave. But how in the heck will we get there?*

Without thinking, Risa spoke, "My horses!"

They all looked at her, eyes wide, as they considered her offer.

More tentatively, Risa asked, "Who knows how to ride?"

Only Lilla raised her hand.

Risa said, "OK, then. I need to teach each of you how to handle and care for a horse."

"Care for?" asked Gemma.

"Yes!" She looked around at their skeptical expressions. "We can do this! My horses will learn to work *with* you, but not for you. Your care will earn their trust." She made no mention of her trip here with a horse that would only go North! "We can use my horse, Sunshine, to train." She silently hoped her horse would agree to go South this time.

Gemma spoke for all of them. "OK then. But how, exactly, do we get to the horses?"

Brit chimed in, "We have one electric car here, and I think there is probably just enough juice to get us to Risa's ranch and her horses."

Satisfied, Gemma offered, "I'll sort out what we will need for our journey. Is it OK, Brit, to use the inventory list we made?"

"Of course."

Finally, somewhat enthusiastic, Lilla said, "Great! While Risa is teaching equestrian skills to you all, I'll start packing up the car with the supplies Gemma chooses."

Misha jumped in, "I can prepare food."

Brit said, "We can work together—that is after I check out the electric charge in the car."

"Wait," came from Risa. "Brit, let me start with you." At Brit's quizzical expression, she said, "Horse training."

"Oh! Yes. Sure. Good idea." *Oh my. This is going so quickly.*

Each left to begin preparations.

* * *

Lilla felt good. Working with Gemma was pleasurable. The sun was warm, just enough spring in the air to produce a cool breeze.

As she carried and then loaded supplies, warm,

peaceful feelings coursed throughout her body. She smiled, trying to remember when she had last felt this way. Goodness—she wasn't mad or upset at anything or anyone.

She stopped working for a spell, to rest her arms. *My boys won't really miss me. They will relish their freedom, and that really is OK. That's different, too!*

* * *

Brit wasn't thrilled about riding a horse, let alone getting close enough to take care of one. However, she knew it was necessary.

Risa put an arm around Brit. "Come on, Brit. You'll love it when you get used to them." She understood Brit's reluctance. However, if she could win over Brit, the others would be easy.

Risa's own love for her horses, along with her confidence, swayed Brit into a more positive attitude. She admired Risa's mount, and how the palomino, Sunshine responded to Risa's subtle movements, seeming to know what was asked of him.

Risa dismounted and said, "OK, Brit. Your turn." She guided Brit as she introduced her to her patient horse.

She had a stool ready to help Brit mount. Seeing how easily Brit actually got on the horse, she was grateful Brit had kept herself so fit.

Once seated, Brit breathed more easily and seemed to enjoy being up so high. Risa led, slowly moving through the pasture that bordered the pine forest. When she turned the reins over to Brit, she was encouraged to see Brit's growing confidence. Risa moved to the side of the horse, letting Brit take the lead.

Risa gave only slight corrections to Brit. *Yes. They were going to be able to do this!*

* * *

Misha explored the food stores. The refrigerator had the basics for sandwiches. She got busy.

She was encouraged by each one's increasingly positive reaction to The Circle. She hadn't been sure about relinquishing her control over the ceremony. *Maybe my ego?* In any case, for each one to take on the lead had resulted in a much stronger group force. They wouldn't be making these preparations otherwise.

Misha laughed at herself as she retrieved lettuce from the greenhouse dome. She had realized—even before the Upheavals—that the ceremony, when done sincerely, brought up problems or issues she was forced to confront head-on. She had finally learned not to run away from them. Interesting how the Elders had not wanted to hear that.

The Circle of Intent, however, was a horse of a different color. Risa would appreciate the reference. She giggled, then paused in her preparations, Risa, and even Lilla, were different since they each had led the group ceremony. There were no more sneers or eye-rolling at every suggestion she made.

She got busy again, packing each sandwich in a plastic bag. She acknowledged that the pressure she had felt leading the Circle lessened as each one stepped up to shoulder that responsibility.

Had she been afraid to let go of leading? Maybe the better word was reluctant. She remembered how she felt when leading or guiding everyone.

Gem was right. How easy it was to want that feeling of power, or Knowing for oneself. She hadn't wanted to share. She stood still, recognizing that her reluctance was a warning sign. That was the 'demon' she thought she had banished.

She finished wrapping the food and put it in the freezer, ready for their journey. She felt an ease, happy.

She knew their Circle was real. Each of them, including herself, could be trusted.

* * *

Gemma efficiently checked off what would be needed for their short car-sprint to Risa's ranch. The longer journey to LA by horseback from the ranch required more careful preparation. She estimated they probably could travel twenty miles a day, assuming they ran into no obstacles. Could they carry enough food, water, tents—or at least some kind of shelter? She wondered if they had enough nutrition packs with them. Maybe Risa had more at the ranch. And what would the horses need?

That Noah hadn't returned weighed on Gemma. Did he even make it to the city? Maybe he had never planned to return. He could have decided that Brit was safe, taken care of, and decided to stay—or maybe he *couldn't* get back. She had known Noah's and Brit's marriage was in trouble.

And if they reached LA, what then? And... Her imagination was working overtime. She had to stop it, or her feeling of being overwhelmed would be contagious, especially for Brit. They could not afford that.

Back to the task at hand. The issue of shelter continued to bother her until she had a brainstorm: her cloak! She had made her own cloak when deciding to walk to find Brit. It had served not only as a wrap but as a blanket, even a kind of shelter when she needed to rest. An image came into her mind of five women on horseback, each wrapped in a different color cloak!

The image was powerful. Who would want to mess with five powerful women on horseback! If that was too conspicuous, they could line them in a neutral color, maybe beige or brown, when they didn't want to be noticed.

All they needed was the cloth to make them.

She had to talk to the others.

CHAPTER 6

Gemma sat at the kitchen table, tapping her nails against the tabletop. As the others came in one by one, they could see Gem's impatience.

"What's up, Gem?" asked Brit.

"The cloaks," she said. "We need to make cloaks—one for each of us, each a different color."

She got puzzled looks from everyone.

"Picture it: the five of us on horseback, riding together with cloaks billowing behind us. Who would think of messing with us?"

Lilla responded, "That certainly would be impressive."

"That is the point, I think," Brit said. "We don't want to threaten anyone. We just want to be left alone. I think it might work."

Risa countered, "Maybe. I hope so. However, if we

don't scare bad people off, let's be prepared with a few basic martial arts moves." She noted their skeptical looks. "I can show you…"

She got a few nods in agreement.

Misha spoke next, "We must not neglect or forget the energy field we are creating through the Circle of Intent. We will be protected if our intent is clear—and united."

"Practically speaking," Lilla said, "Where do we get the cloth for making cloaks? And who knows how to make one?"

"I made my own," said Gemma. "We use my cloak as a pattern. It's pretty simple."

"Sure, why not? If we have cloth," Lilla said.

Brit stopped the impending argument, "Amazing! Once again, Noah to the rescue." She raised her hands, palms out, to stop their questions. "Noah insisted that emergency provisions included bolts of cloth, in the event we had to make our clothes in the future. Well," she said, "the need is here! Come on. I'll show you what we have."

They followed her to a storage room they hadn't seen before. The battery light lit as Brit opened the door.

When Gemma spied the different colored bolts, she exclaimed, "Choose your colors, Ladies!"

Laughing together, they busily examined the many bolts of cloth, each drawn to a color that felt right for her.

Impatient to begin, they used Gemma's turquoise cloak to make a pattern, and soon fell into a routine of marking, cutting, pinning and hand sewing. Creating the beige lining was more challenging since Gemma hadn't lined her own cloak. However, once they figured out how to proceed, their work went quickly.

As Misha worked on her pale-blue cloak, she insisted they continue the Circle ceremony each evening, continuing to alternate who would lead. Working together and finishing each day with the Circle, reinforced their bonding. Misha felt this bonding was as important as all their other preparations if their journey were to be successful.

Brit found that working on the apple green cloth that flattered her fair hair and light complexion and also soothed her anxiety. She had become more anxious the closer they got to leaving. Gemma noticed. She knew Brit still had hopes of returning here with Noah—and the others should they wish to relocate here.

Brit had confessed some of her worries to her: what

if Noah didn't want to come back? She hadn't told anyone about her breakdown. But Gem Knew.

Gemma also knew it was important that Brit unburden herself if their mission were to succeed.

"Come on, Brit. Let's get a cup of tea while we work on these things. I promise I'll help you with the lining."

She drew Brit away from the others, hoping that she would talk to her as they worked.

Once settled and alone together, she urged Brit to tell her everything—for her own sake.

Hesitantly at first, Brit told her about her last fight with Noah: "I felt out of my mind, and I couldn't shake off the awfulness of Noah's accusations. This was while we were still in LA."

She looked up at Gemma and then released all the misery she had been holding back. "He accused me of being brainwashed by the Elders; he said I couldn't see what was right in front of my face. Noah kept telling me that they were corrupt and were corrupting me. He was so furious! He shouted at me: 'Why couldn't I recognize that the earth was speaking, warning us to leave while we could!'"

She stopped. Gem waited.

Finally, Brit went on. "He left and came here to create what he called a safe haven. He said I could come or not! Gemma, he said he had given up trying to reach me. That it was useless."

Brit paused, then broke into a sob, "What *I* felt was that *I* was useless."

Gemma could see that Noah had shocked her into an awakening—if not an understanding.

"And then I crashed," Brit finished. "I couldn't eat. I couldn't move. I slept—I don't know how many days." Through her tears she looked up at Gemma. "Noah found me when he came back to LA."

Neither of them spoke. Gemma just held her as she cried.

Wiping away her tears, she spoke in a subdued tone, "He found me semi-conscious. When I could travel, he brought me up North here to heal. I don't remember very much about that time. That was just days before the 'Big One' hit."

Brit made an effort to gather herself before going on. "We had no way to know how bad it was, aside from rumors gleaned from survivors escaping from the city. Nor did we have any real knowledge of how widespread were the Upheavals.

"I know I told you and the others that he left here to try to find survivors in the city. Truthfully, Noah was deeply concerned about the Gatherers. He said he wanted to know who may have survived the devastation.

"But I know it was me. I wouldn't... *couldn't* talk to him. How do you explain a breakdown?" she said, throwing up her hands in despair.

Gemma felt Brit's misery.

"Finally, the tension and lack of communication between us is what really sent him away—back to Los Angeles."

Gemma wondered how afraid Brit was of finding and then being rejected by him. Whether they agreed about everything or not, Gemma could see that Brit loved him deeply.

Brit gave a deep sigh as she reached for Gemma's hug and reassurance.

CHAPTER 7

Lilla fussed as she worked on her rustic red cloak, "Making these cloaks hasn't turned out to be the easy project Gemma made it seem." She sat back, twisting one black ringlet in her frustration. She scowled and said, "It isn't the colorful side that's hard. It's trying to figure out how to attach the beige lining that's challenging."

Risa chuckled at her complaining.

Lilla glared at Risa. "You're just happy because pumpkin will look gorgeous with your golden palomino."

Risa smiled at Lilla as she came over beside her. "Stop worrying. I'll help you figure it out."

As they continued working on their cloak making project, Misha reminded them that they had to complete the rest of their preparations. Brit advised that they also needed to secure the dome while they were gone.

Gradually, as they worked, their chatter lessened, and even speech became less necessary. They seemed to intuit what needed to be done. Listening became more important, even more interesting as they became aware of their own inner voices and could tune-in to each other.

Misha finally vocalized what they were thinking. "Let's experiment. Let's see if we still are communicating at a distance." There was a shiver that emanated from each of them as they realized that The Shift truly was in them.

Misha knew she could Hear the others from as far away as the pine forest. She was excited that the others were becoming aware that telepathy, at least among the group, was happening.

She still had so many questions about The Shift. However, she felt sure that it would be the ultimate protection for the group.

* * *

Risa continued to instruct each woman with Sunshine, her patient horse. She could see their growing confidence. And as she worked with each woman, she shared her experiences as a lone woman on her ranch, emphasizing how important it had been to know self-defense. One by one, the women accepted her offer to teach them some basics.

After a heated discussion about whether to include guns or rifles on their journey, they compromised. One rifle included—in case they needed to hunt. Risa would instruct those unfamiliar with firearms.

Lilla kept the possession of her own revolver to herself. She wasn't about to be vulnerable to attack, from anything or anyone. She thought Misha had probably tuned in to her determination to keep it a secret. Happily, she didn't seem to be sharing the knowledge with anyone else.

Apparently, it was possible to block mental intrusion. *How does she do that? I have to learn that!*

CHAPTER 8

As the others continued with the preparations, Misha followed Brit.

"Brit?" Misha called. "Can we talk?"

Unaware that she was being followed, Brit was startled. She turned to Misha. "Yes, of course. Always. Where shall we go?" she asked, intuiting that the conversation was to be private.

Misha led her outside and then headed toward the forest. They stopped at the edge near the pines where they found two stumps to sit on.

Brit waited for Misha to begin.

"I know you are concerned about secrets," said Misha.

Brit's heart skipped a beat.

"We need a keeper of secrets. I am willing to do that." Misha waited for Brit to say something. When she didn't, Misha continued, "As we increase our telepathy with each other, fears may arise—like yours —that everything will be known by everyone. It's perhaps the only perceived negative aspect of The Shift." She closely watched Brit's expressions. "Some things may need to be private for the good of the group as well as for each of us."

"Do you know how to block out unwelcome mental intrusion?" asked Brit.

"Not exactly. Not yet. I haven't progressed that far." She took a couple of deep breaths. "That's why the Circle has revealed the possibility for a Keeper of Secrets... And will instruct and monitor that person— until each of us is able to block unwanted transparency."

Brit got up from her stump and slowly began to pace, arms folded across her chest, as she considered Misha's proposal. At last, she stopped, and showing her consternation, she turned to face her. "Doesn't that negate the whole point of telepathy? Absolute transparency is the only way to keep everyone honest. No more lies or manipulation."

Misha appreciated that Brit could put aside her own fears or concerns as she tried to grasp the concept. "Will it help the group to know the details of yours and

Noah's relationship?"

Brit sat again. "So, you already know."

"Yes. As Keeper of Secrets, however, I do not, cannot judge or even empathize. My sole concern is for the good of the group. That's what I am told by the Circle of Intent."

Brit looked intently at Misha as she asked, "How exactly does that work?"

"I don't know how. It just is, and then I come to Know."

"Why you?" Brit asked, keeping her tone as neutral as possible.

Misha smiled in understanding how Brit might question the choice. "I was born a sensitive. I think that's made me very open to The Shift as well as resistant to the manipulations of the Elders."

Brit raised her eyebrows in question.

"It happened when the Elders' fears of losing power overtook their judgment—or their concerns for themselves became more important than the concerns of the Gatherers."

Brit nodded in understanding. "How do we choose what to keep secret?"

"You don't," Misha said. "Nor do I. Somehow, the sorting out is determined by our Circle of Intent—

chosen for the good of the group."

"Then why can't our secrets be held by the Circle? Why is a Keeper of Secrets necessary? No offense. Misha, but that gives enormous power to one person."

Misha hadn't wanted to disclose her own ordeals, but Brit had to understand. "I'm being tested nightly and have been even before coming here. My own Intent is being closely monitored. I think I am just a vehicle for the Circle of Intent; perhaps useful only until we each have mastered how to use The Shift for the good of all."

Brit's facial expression, as well as her body language, showed her grave concern for what Misha was describing. It smelled of Oversight—exactly what the Elders had sought.

"Misha, why are you disclosing this to me—and not to the rest? Let me be plain: I am not interested in Power."

Misha began to answer, but Brit stopped her with a gesture because she needed to puzzle this out.

Did they have a choice? They could cease participating in The Circle of Intent. What would that accomplish? Just leaving them in the same limbo.

A new idea struck Brit. *What if we voluntarily reveal to each other our so-called secrets? That too carried risk. It would either cement or shatter trust among them.*

Brit considered her own secret—about her and Noah. Could she disclose comfortably? Wrong word! After all, she would risk losing the group, her friends. And her breakdown…?

Isolation. That was her fear. And what about knowing their secrets? Could she Hear without judgment?

She knew about Lilla and Noah. She'd learned to compartmentalize in order to lead the group. If everyone knew, could she still embrace Lilla in the same way? She also knew that all of them considered Noah the real leader of the Gatherers. He had the charisma to hold The Gathering together. She did not. Yet, they depended on her, as did Noah, to do the work behind the scenes.

Did she want her resentment and frustration revealed?

She had to stop. Her worries were getting her nowhere.

She Heard Misha's voice in her mind. "I Know. That is why we need the Circle of Intent."

Tears threatened Brit. She realized Misha had Heard or whatever she did. She felt her fear of isolation fading. Obviously, like it or not, she wasn't alone.

Brit pulled herself together and took Misha's hand.

"We need to explore this with everyone—all together."
She squeezed her hand before releasing it. They began
walking together back to the dome.

For the first time, Brit was seeing the dome from a
distance. She gave a short laugh. "It looks like an
enormous egg," she said.

Misha said, "I'd never say that to Noah."

They both laughed as they resumed walking.

Brit was easy, strolling alongside Misha. She had
more confidence in her than before their discussion.
Brit no longer was worried about her motives. She
neither felt nor sensed any self-aggrandizement from
Misha.

However, as she thought about the others, she wasn't
sure how they would respond. She realized Misha was
unsure as well. Could they accept a Keeper of Secrets?
Just the title made Brit shudder.

Perhaps she should take the lead. Maybe take each
one aside. No, that just set up the same fear dynamic
fostered by the Elders. Misha or anyone else holding all
their secrets would not sit well with any of them.

Mainly, she was hesitant about confronting Lilla. Brit
had never revealed what she knew about Noah and
Lilla. *Will I ever be able to think outside of that box?*
She remonstrated with herself: *discussion does not*

mean confrontation!

She shook her head. They had reached the dome, but both were still undetermined about the next step.

CHAPTER 9

Brit wanted to gather everyone together after dinner. Misha persuaded her to do it after that evening's Circle. Brit reluctantly agreed, knowing she just wanted the discussion to be over.

Following the Circle ceremony, the women once again gathered around the kitchen table, wondering what was up now. They all had picked up on Brit's intensity.

She thanked them for their hard work with preparations, securing the dome, and participating in the Circle. "It's the Circle of Intent we must discuss before we move forward."

There were nervous looks all round. Then backs straightened as everyone felt the more serious energy.

Gemma asked, "Has something new happened?" The others murmured the same question.

"Misha has Heard that we may need a 'Keeper of Secrets.'"

There was silence. And then Lilla said, "A what?!"

Brit hurriedly cut off further questions. As simply as she could, she said, "We each have secrets or at least private concerns we would prefer not to broadcast to the world, or even to each other. The problem is that we don't know how to block unwanted mental intrusion. And until we learn, according to what Misha has Heard, she can be a sort of mental vault that holds those secrets."

Brit glanced at Misha and gestured an apology for designating her that way. Misha smiled and nodded her OK. The others were murmuring again. Before they erupted into full debate mode, Brit signaled her wish to continue speaking.

"I presented another possible solution. We each could voluntarily disclose any secret or issue that has the potential to disrupt or even destroy the group's unity."

She paused and looked for feedback from each woman. "That would prevent anyone from attempting to have…" She searched for a neutral word, but Gemma said it for her. "Power. No one person would have power over anyone else."

Lilla pushed herself from the table. "I, for one, want

no part of either *solution*. Who gives Misha the power to know everything about everybody?"

Brit stepped toward Lilla, then hesitated as Risa spoke up, "Maybe all this 'Circle' stuff is a mistake."

Gemma huffed, "It's not like we can just turn off The Shift or opt-out. It's real. It's here. It's why we all are here."

At last, Misha spoke up, "The key to all this is in our intent."

The women turned their focus to Misha, who read their distrust and skepticism. She pleaded, "We are so close to realizing our Intent. Our power as a group will expand exponentially once our mutual intent is fully revealed."

"Revealed?" said Brit. "By what? By whom?" Brit's aggressive tone drew everyone's attention to her. But they quickly turned back to Misha. They wanted an answer.

At first, Misha seemed to crumple in her chair, trying to disappear. But she rallied, took a deep breath, and stood her ground. "The Intent," she emphasized, "comes from us. It's determined by us. And it must be a consensus."

She leaned into the table, her body taut with her effort to make them understand. "Each of us was compelled to come here, at the same time, to be together. None of us knew why. The 'Circle of Intent' drew us here to activate the intention. Please believe me; this is not about me. It's about us becoming a force for good. It brought us together; It will bring others." She leaned back, emotionally exhausted by their wrangling, their fear.

Gemma moved and stood behind Misha. She put her hands on her shoulders. "Misha has spoken for the Circle of Intent. It's up to us to either reject both the circle and Misha or to honor Misha's efforts to unite us, especially by reactivating the ceremony. We have to acknowledge the reality and the power of The Shift, for good or bad. How are we going to use it?"

Lilla flounced up and quickly exited.

The others watched her leave but didn't move.

Lilla pulled her things from the closet and dresser drawers. She was headed back to her summer cabin and to her boys. She threw her clothes into her duffel and slammed shut the drawers once they were empty.

Angry feelings raged through her. Her fears were nobody's business but hers. How dare they lull everyone with how wonderful and full of promise was

The Shift? *All lies!* It was terrible to think she would have to live in isolation to escape its power. *Ugh! She hated it.*

Brit was the first to move. She intuited Lilla's objective. She pulled Risa aside, "Do you know what Lilla is planning?"

Risa said, "I think she has already left."

"Would you go after her? You are closer to her than the rest of us."

"I'm not sure that will help. But sure. I'll try." Risa left.

As she focused, Risa could feel Lilla's fear and anxiety. No need, she thought. So unnecessary. *We are all in this together.* Risa's own intent grew as she approached Lilla.

Fortunately, Lilla hadn't got very far, and she quickly became aware of a warmth flooding through her. Who was doing that? She Saw that Risa was coming after her, which surprised her. She was convinced she was totally alone. She could not accept that someone cared about her or would even come after her, certainly not Risa. She tried to reject the mental intrusion. It persisted.

Risa continued to 'tune-in' to Lilla's confusion. She wanted to reassure her to make her less afraid. She could feel that she was getting closer to her, and at last, she caught sight of her.

Her own feelings surprised Risa. She cared and hoped Lilla would come back with her and join the others. It was so important to determine together their next steps. She found she liked this difference in herself.

Lilla was aggravated that she felt the bonds holding her to the group. Worse! It was also comforting. *How could that be true?* What kept her from returning with Risa? *Her pride! Everyone would know what she felt.*

Risa had quickly caught up with Lilla. She reached out to touch her arm. "You'll know how everyone else is feeling too!"

Lilla Felt more than Heard her words, as she accepted Risa's embrace. Tears coursed down Lilla's cheeks as she let herself be turned around. Together they went down the path she had just taken. Risa's arm around her was so comforting.

CHAPTER 10

As Risa prepared for bed, she mulled over Lilla's extreme reaction to the idea of disclosing. Risa never dwelt on the past. What was the point? It didn't change anything. She was content with her horses and quietly realized how much she missed her ranch.

Her dad had trusted her to take care of the ranch and the animals. So lucky. Although Risa had felt the lure of the Big City, she had never completely left her home. *What if I hadn't been there to take over when Dad got sick?*

Even when Jake entered the picture and introduced her to some wonderful people in what was called The Gathering, she couldn't abandon her horses or her dad.

Handsome Jake had made The Gathering Community sound like Utopia.

Ha! Not exactly! The closer she got to The Gathering,

the clearer it became that his idea of Utopia certainly wasn't hers. Jake had embraced the practice of many women to one man. *The Elders encouraged it!* When she asked whether one woman could have several men, however, they let her know she was very naïve. *Humiliating!*

How did Noah and Brit manage it? Maybe they didn't. And maybe she didn't want to know their secrets.

Risa shook off those memories and climbed into bed. She was surprised at herself—going after Lilla—and her success in bringing her back. It had always been difficult to get close to Lilla. You never knew what sharp retort might come your way.

One time, Risa had made a snide remark about Jake. Before she could explain her feelings, Lilla retorted that she was stupid to ever trust a man. Risa backed off. Yet, tonight she had responded to Lilla's obvious need for a friend. Her eyelids drooped as she snuggled into the covers.

The men who had claimed to be in love with Risa were very obviously looking for a free ride—and not on her horses. She smothered a giggle. Anyway, Risa gave up looking for the 'right' man.

Maybe that is what she sensed about Lilla. She knew

that they had both experienced abuse. Differently maybe, but still…

Anyway, she was glad Lilla had come back with her. Risa wasn't ready for her group to disband. Sleep overtook her.

* * *

Gemma saw Misha leave for the outdoors and decided to follow her at a distance. She watched her heading for the circle of stones and decided to leave her be. The group was clearly at a crossroads. The issue of trust was huge. She wasn't ready to go back into the dome. The slightest breeze lifted her auburn hair as she strolled the path that circled the dome. So many memories!

Gemma felt progress was made after each ceremony. Her instinct told her that The Shift was benign. She had waited for this ever since joining The Gathering. She didn't exactly Hear as Misha did. She simply Knew that her own senses dramatically shifted as the Upheavals grew in strength. She no longer vaguely sensed; she Knew.

She trusted what Misha Heard and Gem Knew their

group was going in the right direction. If full disclosure would solidify the group's power, that was fine with her.

Her own 'secret'? She knew the group would accept, but maybe not Brit. It was Brit she felt drawn to. Would she understand or feel threatened? Gemma felt very protective over Brit and would give her life to protect her if it came to that.

From her youth, Gemma had ambivalent feelings about sex. Whether a man or woman, she simply followed her feelings. She knew that wasn't what she wanted from Brit. Their companionship, their mutual trust is what she was determined to protect. The Gathering had fulfilled her, especially as she had accepted leadership with Brit. These special women were the core of the larger group they had in LA. She did not want to disband. Not now, when they were so close to becoming One.

The Elders had been her nemesis. She had managed to avoid them until they started micromanaging the groups. She was severely reprimanded when Brit left without requesting permission. They made Gemma responsible for the dissolution of their group. She felt Brit's absence keenly. After all, Brit was the one with diplomatic talents.

As the earth's rumblings increased, Gem Knew it was time to leave, but she never got it together until the Big One hit. As her home crumbled around her, she was literally thrown out by the Universe.

Without knowing exactly where the 'family' summer cabin was, she loaded up her personal belongings that survived and drove North. She had no choice but to trust the growing certainty of her Knowing.

The major aftershock to the 'Big One' hit the day after she found the cabin. She found it just in time. She was grateful there was minimal damage to the small structure. She was safe for the moment. The aftershocks were unsettling, but her parents had built well. The small three-room cabin suited her fine.

Gemma had not been ready for the growing compulsion to find Brit. But at last, she left, once more trusting her Knowing. She recalled her conversation with Noah. He had confided to her his plan to build a dome house. That would serve as her goal—find the dome house!

She had no idea how Brit would respond to her showing up on her doorstep—if there was a doorstep! Before the Upheavals, when she tried to talk to Brit about how unhappy she was with the Elders, Brit had yelled at her, and then very uncharacteristically dissolved into tears. And then she simply disappeared without a word. Gemma simply did not Know what had happened to Brit or Noah.

Was she ready to disclose her own secrets? Absolutely, if it would protect the unity of their Circle.

CHAPTER 11

Brit was the only one left in the kitchen, her elbows on the table, her head in her hands. She felt numb. Exhausted by so many unanswered questions. She certainly didn't have solutions.

Was the group finished? How would each one survive on her own? And what about her?

At this point, she was ready to disclose anything they wanted to know. Protecting their secrets just felt petty to her. So what if they knew about her failed marriage? *I'm done pretending, and certainly not for Noah's sake. Or for mine.*

Pride. Useless. No one is going to lead anyone— certainly not me. If someone wants to be the leader, well, let them try.

She left the table. All she wanted was sleep. Tomorrow? Who knows?

* * *

Noah came again into Brit's dream time. This time he spoke, and she could hear him.

"You are needed here," he said. "I want you here—with me. Our work together is needed. So many need us."

"Do *you* want me?" she asked, hoping.

Her heartbeat accelerated. Tears flooded her eyes, and she woke, coughing up the phlegm that was choking her. She was confused as she raised herself and sat with her head against the headboard. *The dream was so real. No. It was a message!*

She glanced at the clock beside her bed. Way too early, still dark outside. Nevertheless, sleep was out of the question. She decided there was no point in staying in bed.

Oh, how she would love a cup of coffee!

* * *

Sleep, the great healer! *Whoever said that?* Gemma felt optimistic this morning. *Hopefully, everyone will have processed everything that went down last night. They might even realize that they have very little choice!* Time to get herself out of bed.

Gemma was relieved that Lilla had come back to them. Risa surprised her. Gem was encouraged by her growth. It was a further validation that The Shift was benign. She would talk with everyone. Surely she could get them all on the same page.

When she got to the kitchen area, she was happy to find the kettle hot. She needed a strong cup of tea.

Risa told her that Misha had got a cup and gone out on the patio. Lilla was still asleep. She hadn't seen Brit yet this morning.

Gemma sat down next to Risa, who indicated a desire to talk.

"Gem, do you think we can leave soon?"

Gem tilted her head and shrugged that she couldn't say.

"I'm concerned about my horses. Besides, we need to get to the ranch to continue training. Before we start for LA. It's important for each of us to bond with our own horse."

Gem smiled encouragement. "We still have to make a decision about the Circle, and whether we go forward or backward."

Risa sat back. "I agree with you. We really have no choice. Everything is coming out whether we talk or tune-in. No one knows—at least yet—how to block."

Lilla appeared, still sleepy. She waved hello to Risa and Gem. "Is the water hot?"

Gem got up. "I'll make you a cup of tea. Come on, have a seat." She pulled out a chair for her.

Brit bustled in, got a cup of tea, and refilled the kettle and put it back on the burner. "I think we should leave for Risa's ranch as soon as possible."

Gem smiled, Risa's mouth flew open, and Lilla just stared at Brit.

"We're prepared," she continued. "The journey to the ranch will give us a look at what we may face once we're traveling on horseback."

Brit sat, sipping her tea. The others began nodding in agreement.

"I intend to get to Los Angeles even if I have to walk," said Brit. They gaped at her as they took in her declaration.

Finally, Gem asked, "What's happening, Brit?"

Brit took a breath, considering what to share. Then she laughed at herself. "Can't you tell?" she asked, looking at each one.

As it dawned on them, they laughed with her.

"Apparently, it takes effort to tune-in," said Gemma.

"Good to know," said Risa.

Brit decided to confide in them, "I had a dream. Actually, it was more than a dream. It was a message from Noah."

Gem and Risa both showed their eagerness to hear. Lilla withdrew and stared into her cup.

Brit noticed. "I know about you and Noah, Lilla. Please—just let it go." She reached her arms out in an invitation to Lilla.

Lilla's face lost all color. She tried to speak, but the words wouldn't come.

"Please," said Brit. She reached Lilla and pulled her into an embrace.

She turned to the others. "We have to face that we are opening to each other. If we can't handle that, there is no point in continuing."

No one noticed that Misha had joined them.

Risa was the first to see her and rose to bring her into the group.

"Well?" asked Lilla, wondering where Misha was in all this.

"You all will decide. I've made my peace with The

Circle of Intent."

They were quiet, watching Misha sit down.

Gemma brought her a cup of tea. "We are waiting to Hear Noah's message," she said. "He spoke to Brit last night in a dream."

"Yes, I know," Misha said. "Please share it with us, Brit."

Brit said, "He wants me—us—to come. He needs us." She teared up, "This is the first time I've been able to Hear him."

They each felt her vulnerability and her longing. This was the first time Brit had revealed herself to them. Each felt the tug on their own hearts, opening in response.

"I'm so sorry, Brit," Lilla said.

Brit gave her a sad smile. "I know," she said. She got up to turn off the screeching kettle. "More tea?" she asked.

CHAPTER 12

Preparations were quickly completed. The electric car was fully charged. Brit hoped that it wasn't overloaded with passengers and supplies. Breaking down before getting to the ranch would be very unfortunate.

Before they piled into the car, they tried their cloaks. Together, they agreed, they would present a colorful, even imposing presence. An energetic vibration surrounded their activities. Their happy camaraderie was infectious. There seemed no need for further discussion.

Each woman was aware that they were committed to going forward together. Learning that it took an effort to tune-in to others as well as to block—although how to block was still a mystery—was reassuring. It alleviated the feeling of powerlessness. For now, it was enough.

Brit and Gem took a final walk around the dome, making sure it was secure.

"Noah was so wise," said Brit. Seeing the question on Gem's face, she said, "The ways he insured the dome could almost take care of itself. When—if—we return, it will be here, ready for us."

Gem nodded her understanding.

Brit stopped walking and took Gem's arm. "Gem. I Know. You have nothing to fear. In my own way, I love you dearly." Brit maintained eye contact with Gem until she saw the relief and appreciation in her face.

"Thank you. I wasn't sure."

"Come on. The others will be impatient," said Brit as she hurried them to the loaded car. "Good thing we're only four of us in the car," she said when they reached the others. Risa had taken off on her horse before dawn. Lilla had commented on how happy she seemed to be headed home.

Brit got the car moving slowly until she was reassured all was well. She and Gem had agreed to trade off driving. They decided to not make a stop until they caught up with Risa.

Misha sat up front next to the driver. She maintained her meditative energy in order to navigate the damaged roads and monitor their progress. Lilla and Gem were in the back seat, squeezed between supplies and luggage.

At the ranch, the plan was to finish their training with the horses. And depending on conditions they saw on their way to the ranch, make educated guesses on how best to proceed. They soon discovered that their journey was likely to be slow. The land was open range. Cattle and other animals moved freely, often on the only paved road.

Suddenly, Lilla called out that there was danger up ahead. No one saw anything dangerous until the car got to the top of a small rise in the road. Below them were hundreds of sheep meandering along the road.

More important, was the discovery that Lilla was hyper-sensitive to energy that suggested danger. Gem, who was driving, thanked her warmly, expressing how beneficial this could be to all of them. Her newfound talent might even help them avoid unsavory people.

Again, Brit silently thanked Noah for his choice of an off-road car, because that was the only way they were going to get around the animals.

For the first time in many months, Brit felt assured and clear about her direction. She stopped worrying about Noah and her relationship. It was enough that she was needed. There must be survivors of the Gathering —mustn't there be? Wasn't that Noah's implied message? It had to be a message—dream or no dream. She just Knew. The car started bouncing along a rough piece of the road, evidence of serious earthquake damage. Luckily, Brit was jolted from her daydreaming in time to see the large boulder in the middle of the road. She focused on finding an alternative path around it as well as avoiding the fissures breaking up the earth. Mini-quakes had been so frequent, they almost had stopped noticing them. On the road, inattention could be dangerous.

Brit and Gem both voiced their uncertainty about how much further they had to drive. They hadn't yet caught up with Risa. She must have found her way. Risa had assured them they would reach the ranch before heading into the mountain pass which they could see in the distance.

Their progress was slower now. They passed a few cars, apparently abandoned. No point in hurrying and then breaking down. Happily, Lilla sensed nothing to alarm them. Not knowing how far they had yet to travel was unnerving.

More training in trusting was Gem's hope.

The first evidence that they were close was the fencing and the sight of two magnificent horses, one black as night. The other was Risa's palomino! Both were grazing in the distant meadow. Loud releases of pent-up tensions along with sighs of gratitude expressed their relief. But where was the ranch? Brit's eyes kept sweeping over the landscape. Finally, she glimpsed smoke rising from a distant ranch house.

The sound of the approaching car must have reached the building. There was Risa, waving vigorously at them to come on in!

They'd made it! First goal—done.

CHAPTER 13

Rounding a curve in the road, they got their first good look at the red-tiled roof of the ranch house. They could see that it was one long structure: the main house in the center was flanked by smaller rooms on either side. Each room had a door that led outside onto a veranda that wrapped around the entire building. A short distance from the main structure was a barn. Next to that was a corral, no doubt for the horses.

Risa came off the veranda, running to meet their car, which circled in front of the main building before coming to a stop. The women happily got out of the cramped car to embrace Risa.

Two young men came to help unload the car, stacking everything on the veranda awaiting instructions. Risa directed them to take the supplies into the kitchen and leave the luggage for later.

Once Risa showed everyone the big room with its fireplace, easy chairs, and sofa, she got drinks for everyone from the attached kitchen. Figuring that they must be weary, she suggested they retrieve their luggage, and then she would show them to their rooms. She explained that the rooms on the north side were for the people who worked here on her ranch or for refugees on their way North. The rooms on the south side of the main room were reserved for her friends.

As Risa led them along the long corridor, she designated which room each woman would occupy. Her room was next to the main one, then Brit's, Gem's, Lilla's, and lastly, Misha's. She indicated that there was a door in each room that led out onto the veranda. Both doors could be locked from the inside.

Before Misha entered her room, she drew Risa aside. "I'd like to find the best place for our evening Circle."

Risa nodded, understanding, but hesitated. "Why don't we wait until everyone is settled." But seeing that Misha was becoming agitated, she said, "Come on. Let's talk in here." She ushered her into the room.

Misha was puzzled but followed her.

"There are other people here on the property," Risa began. "Finding a place away from prying eyes may be difficult."

"Let them join us," Misha responded.

"Is that wise?"

"It could accomplish a lot," said Misha.

"Like what?"

Misha said, "Show we have nothing to hide." Misha sat on the edge of the bed, testing the springs. "Maybe gain their support." She looked up at Risa. "Make it clear to *us* that The Shift and our Gathering is benign."

"*Please*—we are *not* the Gathering!"

"We have to call ourselves something," Misha rejoined.

"The Shifters?" Risa joked. "I don't know. Just anything but The Gathering."

"OK. We'll ask the group—or the Circle. So, where shall we perform our ceremony?"

Hearing the others outside on the veranda, Risa opened the outside door and motioned to them to join her and Misha.

Risa said to the group, "We have a problem to solve —about holding the Circle."

Misha said, "Risa explained that there are others on the ranch. They may be curious, or possibly even threatened by the ceremony. I suggest that we invite anyone who wishes to join us."

"Oh Brother!" came from Lilla, obviously disturbed

by that idea.

Brit and Gem looked at each other, hoping to Know where the other stood.

Brit quickly offered her opinion before Lilla could comment further. "Why not? Maybe this is part of our intent." She looked at Risa and then Lilla. "We have nothing to hide. It could reassure everyone that we aren't doing something sinister."

Gem said, "We have to test our strength, our *power*, sometime! Good. Now is good."

Misha smiled her appreciation. "All that's left then is the place," she said, turning to Risa.

Risa acquiesced, "Anywhere then is fine."

* * *

Risa turned her thoughts to the horses as the others went inside to settle in. How would they decide who would ride which horse? She was glad the women had taken to riding enthusiastically. But it was important to match rider and horse correctly.

She was delighted Carlos had decided to stay. He had appeared on her doorstep shortly after the big shocks and Upheavals had begun. Her eyes had been opened by him to the unique intelligence of horses. He was truly a horse whisperer.

As she approached the door to her room, Carlos stopped her. "Ms. Risa. Are we ready for the horses?"

Before answering, she stood, considering until she felt the pull. "Just one, Carlos. The black stallion."

"Will you be riding him, ma'am?"

"No, Carlos." She motioned him to walk with her. "I want to introduce Diablo to Brit."

She then sat in the wicker rocker and indicated that he should take the chair beside her.

From his followers, she had learned that Carlos was from a long line of medicine men, shamans. She fully trusted his judgment. Would he trust hers?

"I can't explain why I think this is a good fit—and maybe it isn't. But I trust Diablo to know." She wasn't surprised at his puzzled, perhaps concerned reaction. She knew how special he believed the black stallion to be.

She looked at him as he stared into her eyes, which created an energy both felt. As he held her eyes, he said nothing. She did not flinch or look away.

At last, he gave a slight nod, rose to leave, and said, "I will bring Diablo now."

Risa returned his nod and went inside to prepare Brit.

At the knock on her outside door, Brit called, "Come in."

Risa came in, saying, "I want to introduce you to our black stallion, Diablo." Seeing the uncertain look on Brit's face, she added, smiling, "It's just an introduction."

"Diablo—not *too* intimidating," said Brit. "Why me? I mean, he's huge! I'm just learning to enjoy riding."

"So, you've seen him?" Risa smiled as she hooked her arm in Brit's and opened the outside door. From the veranda, they observed Carlos leading the splendid animal toward them.

"This is my horse trainer and foreman—and friend, Carlos," Risa said. "He joined me with his people after the big shocks, and the Upheavals began." She turned to him, "Carlos, this is Ms. Brit." She walked down the stairs to greet him and Diablo.

Brit was awed by the black stallion, his regal appearance. Almost unwillingly, she was drawn to him and, without thinking, moved to him and put her hand on his flanks.

He stood very still. When she removed her hand, he turned his head toward her. He seemed to be studying her.

Carlos watched carefully. Both he and Risa were surprised at Diablo's immediate acceptance. They seemed to belong together. Carlos put his hands on the horse's nose, looking and feeling his energy.

Finally, he turned to Risa and gave a short nod. "I will work with both of them."

Risa let out the breath she had been holding before nodding back. She then turned to Brit, "Meet your new partner."

* * *

Early the next day, while enjoying their morning coffee on the veranda, Carlos gave Risa his report about the ranch while she had been away. After Risa's questions had been answered and plans for the day had been made, Carlos suggested that all the women be invited to choose a horse. Risa lifted one eyebrow. She knew that each horse would do the choosing.

Carlos told her that their gentle gray mare had taken off again. He had looked for her, but she was still missing. He intended to search for her this morning.

Risa agreed but asked him to hold off until the

choosing had taken place. When Carmella brought them more coffee, Risa asked her to wake the women and ask them to join her on the veranda as soon as they were dressed. Risa then directed Carmella to bring coffee for everyone.

When they all had gathered, she pointed to the horses that were milling about in front of the veranda. She suggested that they focus their intent to find their mount. She told them that Brit had been assigned the black stallion which they saw her leading into the nearby pasture.

"You can watch the horses while you wake up with some coffee." She smiled. The women responded to the word 'coffee' with enthusiasm.

The women showed their nervousness, not sure what they should—or shouldn't—be doing.

"What exactly should we be watching for?" asked Lilla.

"You'll know," said Risa.

There were several horses to choose from. Risa was fascinated to see the 'dance.' As a woman approached one horse, it would either welcome her or shy away. The only horse Gemma was allowed to come close to was Ginger, a sweet-tempered horse the color of rust. At first, it moved away, but then abruptly turned back and walked directly to the delighted Gemma.

Risa saw that the chestnut, Blaze—named for the white marking on his forehead—seemed to tease Lilla. He came up behind her, nosed her back, then quickly trotted off. Lilla stumbled, then shouted her surprise as she regained her balance. Irritated, she spun around, ready to berate the obnoxious creature who was trotting away from her. When she went after him, he galloped away, making a large circle around the group until he arrived back and stood beside her.

Lilla stood with hands on her hips and began laughing at him. He snorted back at her, but he didn't move away.

Misha hadn't moved. She stood, eyes closed, waiting. After several minutes, she opened her eyes and began slowly walking a path through the milling horses until she came to the edge of the pasture.

Everyone stopped to watch her. In the distance, they saw Brit with the black stallion. But beyond her, they could see a gray blur coming toward them. The blur soon took shape as the gray mare galloped across the green meadow, heading straight for Misha. The mare didn't slow until she came close and then halted before Misha. Misha extended her hand to touch her.

"Cloud. Your name is Cloud," Misha said to her.

Cloud took one more step toward Misha and then bent her head to accept her touch.

Everyone, including Carlos and Risa, was spellbound as they watched what seemed a sacred ceremony taking place before them.

Carlos rose, bowed to Risa, and left the women to become acquainted with their new partners—and friends.

After a long afternoon of training with their new partners, the ladies were ready for a shower, lunch, and a nap.

Risa went inside to oversee the preparations for their dinner. She wanted to celebrate; she wanted a banquet! There might not be another opportunity.

She ordered the linens for the long table and had the silver brought out and polished. Candles were already used each evening.

One of the young women shyly asked if she could bring in flowers for decorations. Risa was delighted with her suggestion.

Risa wasn't sure what they were celebrating—maybe their survival. Whatever the reason, she felt light-hearted. It had been such a long time since anyone celebrated anything. It was truly a joyful gathering. She sighed; that word again! Well, it was a gathering. She'd just have to accept it.

CHAPTER 14

Before sunset, Risa called everyone to the main room. Many oohs and aahs were heard as each person arrived and saw the table decorated with flowers intertwined into vine garlands. The linens, silverware, and china plates reflected the candlelight. Great care had been taken to transform a simple meal into a banquet.

Risa addressed everyone. "Misha suggested that our Circle should be here tonight, around the table. Those who have created such a beautiful table and prepared our food have been invited to join us." She turned and spoke to them. "Please, if you wish, blend your voices with ours as we create harmony."

Surprised, but happy with this invitation, the five women and those who joined them began by holding hands around the table.

Brit suddenly realized she knew their intent. She spoke: "We survive to serve." The women echoed the words. Then everyone joined as the mantra was repeated.

Risa then began the hum which was immediately taken up harmoniously by the women. As the hum grew in strength, it evolved into a bell-like tone, and then resounded as some observers joined. Joyful harmony embraced them. It seemed without beginning or end.

Then, with one voice, the toning became quieter and then ceased. One breath was taken by the group and released slowly as they all opened their eyes. No words were spoken. Smiles expressed it all.

As Risa sat, inviting everyone to join her, the servers scurried to the kitchen to bring out the platters of freshly picked vegetables steamed in a savory sauce. The freshly baked bread and newly churned butter were placed on the table. Another brought in the homemade jam. Ice tea was poured into their glasses. The simple meal felt like a feast. The servers then sat and joined in the festivities.

Although very tired from the long, eventful day, Brit tossed and turned in her bed. She marveled at their amazing journey. She reflected on all the preparations they had done together to bring them here.

Her connection to Diablo—and her amazement at her discovery that they communicated! Not in words exactly, more in Knowing, It was beyond understanding.

And then her Knowing the Intent—to serve. It seemed so simple, maybe too simple—but it wasn't.

She closed her eyes as she tried to puzzle it out—and finally slept.

CHAPTER 15

The deep underground rumblings of the earth made the horses restless. The night calls of birds ceased. The rhythmic song of the cicadas abruptly stopped. The howls of the coyotes no longer filled the night air.

The stillness was unsettling. Carlos emerged from his quarters and walked among the horses, reassuring the gray mare, Cloud, with a hand on her flank, a soft word to Ginger and Blaze, and a shushing sound to calm Diablo. Risa's palomino, Sunshine, took a few moments of stroking to settle.

Carlos readied himself for what he sensed was coming.

And then it came: A thunderous sound from violent churning movements of the earth. The ground rolled beneath his feet, upsetting his balance. He regained it and stumbled to the barn door.

He heard crashing sounds coming from inside the ranch house. As he got to the screen door, the house shook and continued shaking. He knew the inhabitants would be terrified, but he couldn't check on everyone until the quake finally stopped. At last, the heaving earth was still, and the clanging of the pots and pans ceased.

Gemma untangled herself from the sheets in her tossed-about bed. She wanted to check that everyone was all right. They all emerged from their rooms into the hallway unscathed, if rattled.

Without saying anything, they headed through the main room into the hallway connecting the rooms in the north wing of the house. They found everyone shaken and scared but not hurt.

The main room had survived without damage as far as they could tell. Gemma commented, "Thank heaven that no candles were burning."

Carlos came in, looking for Risa. She assured him that all the people had survived with only minor scratches. He let her know that all the animals were unhurt and were once again bedded down in the barn.

Since dawn was still at least two hours away, he

suggested it might be wise if everyone stayed in the main room in case of strong aftershocks.

Just as he spoke, a sudden jolt shook the house. No one panicked, but there were many deep breaths.

Risa with Brit advised people to get a blanket and pillow from their rooms and try to find a spot in the main room where they could lie down and try to get some rest.

The women gathered their cloaks and bedded down on the soft carpet. Their respite from worry was at an end.

As sun rays came through the front windows, the tension in the room eased. Some of the workers gathered up their blankets and pillows and went back to their rooms.

Two of the older women started heating hot water for tea. Risa took Carmella aside and asked her to retrieve from the emergency storeroom coffee—and make sure there was enough for everyone.

Carmella, who had arrived with Carlos' group, had been given charge of the kitchen. She was delighted to go after the coffee.

It didn't take long for the aroma of freshly brewed

coffee to permeate the room, lifting everyone's spirits. And as breakfast appeared on the long table, the atmosphere became much happier. They could even try to ignore the few sudden tremors.

Risa put a mug into Carlos' hands when he entered the room. She got her own cup and joined him to investigate what might need repairs.

After making the rounds, they determined that very little had been damaged. The hired hands would watch for the crevasses that cut through the pasture, where they exercised the horses. Once the animals became aware of the shifted earth, they would be safer.

"I am so relieved and grateful," Risa expressed to Carlos as they walked the pasture. She wondered whether their Circle of Intent had protected them.

Carlos was aware of her unasked question. He put a hand on her arm, and they stopped. In his quiet way, he said, "Ms. Risa. We have our Circle too." He referred to the men and women who had accompanied him to the ranch. "You have given us refuge, even friendship. How could we not offer our protection to you?"

Risa was stunned at this revelation.

"Our Circle and your Circle are the same, although different. Together we have created a powerful energy field of protection." He opened his arms as he looked all around them before he gazed at Risa once again.

"What you call The Shift, we together have harnessed."

With that comment, he gave her a slight bow and walked quickly to his quarters.

* * *

"We have to talk." Risa found Brit helping to clear the main room.

"OK. What do we have to—" began Brit.

"Alone. With the others. Privately."

Brit could see the urgency on her face. "I'll gather the others. My room?"

"Good."

Within a few minutes, the women seated themselves in Brit's small room, wondering what was coming next.

Risa told them about her conversation with Carlos.

Lilla asked, "What does he mean? His Circle and our Circle are the same?"

"I'm not exactly sure," said Risa

"Who is he anyway? I mean, he is damned fine looking, and I won't ask whether you and he…" Lilla's eyebrows were raised in question, a little smirk on her face.

"Oh please!" said Risa. He is old enough to be my father. He is a wise man—even a shaman.

"Well, I don't think he is *that* old," said Gemma. "He can't be over fifty, and a fine specimen at that. He certainly knows horses."

Misha looked at each of them, puzzled. "It's clear to me that he is a shapeshifter."

Lilla exclaimed, "A what?"

Brit stopped her with a gesture. "Except I don't think he is the one shifting his shape. I think how he looks or what he says is different for each of us. Maybe he projects a different image to each of us, dependent on what each of us is looking for." She shrugged. "I don't know. I've never experienced anything like this."

Risa listened to what everyone was saying, thinking back to how he had come to the ranch...

The Upheavals had stopped Risa from returning to Los Angeles. Her ranch had stayed intact, even after the Big One hit. After a few weeks, she was pretty sure she was on her own. She had no idea how she was going to proceed.

From time to time, she thought about Jake, a would-be cowboy she had met at The Gathering. He had surprised her, one day arriving at her ranch uninvited.

Cocky! For sure. Of course, she was attractive to him, a woman on her own with a ranch she owned! She had sent him on his way rather quickly. That was before the Mega-quake. Otherwise, she might have been tempted.

One morning, after that encounter with Jake, Risa saw a small group of men, women, and children, approaching the ranch on foot. They wore colorful serapes and interesting head covers. The man she came to know as Carlos was clearly the one in charge.

Carlos asked if they could camp on the land. They had traveled for many days, and the women and children were beginning to suffer from exhaustion.

Risa's heart reached out to the children, and she told them they could stay as long as they wished.

That was the beginning of their relationship. The men had seen what needed to be done on the land, and Carlos made sure each of the horses was in good health.

The helpful women made her own chores almost disappear. She became calm, even with the quakes. She felt safe.

As for Misha's assertion that Carlos was a shapeshifter—she didn't even try to understand.

CHAPTER 16

The days and weeks passed quickly. Carlos and his men helped the women become one with their horses. Each woman was discovering an intuitive communication between horse and rider.

The women were also instructed in special food preparations for their journey and fire building skills. They also learned different ways they could utilize their cloaks. Shelter was possible by putting them side by side in a circle.

It was Carmella who suggested using the different colors as a banner when riding together and using the same-colored lining side for disguise.

Many of Carlos group asked if they could join their Circle each evening. They were warmly welcomed.

* * *

A young man from Carlos' group came galloping toward the barn. He quickly dismounted and handed the reins to one of the boys with instructions to cool down the horse. He ran to find Carlos.

After hearing the report, Carlos found Risa, chatting with Gemma.

"Many refugees are coming from Los Angeles after the last big shock. According to some, the roads are almost gone.

"Even more disturbing are reports of roving gangs who are robbing and terrorizing travelers. Women may not be safe on the trail."

Risa asked, "Gemma, please find the others."

Brit was the most distressed by the news. However, she was anxious to continue their journey in spite of objections from Lilla and Risa. They argued how much safer they were here on the ranch, especially with the company of Carlos and his people. It was hard to dispute their concerns. This latest news made it even less attractive to move on.

Misha tried to redirect them to the Circle. In what ways they should include Carlos' group was still being discussed. Many of Carlos' group were already joining in the song-without-words. Brit pointed out that combining the Circles was never an option. According to Carlos, they had their own Circle, although their intent was similar to their own.

Misha asked, "Why can't they join us and still have their own Circle as well?"

That seemed the most reasonable suggestion.

Risa brought them back to the main question, "What is so urgent about getting to LA?"

"Noah," said Brit, "and whoever he may have found."

"Our intent is to serve," Gem added. "Not to hole up in hopes that we'll be OK."

Lilla interjected, "What does their Circle want?"

They all looked at her.

"It can't hurt to ask," she said.

Brit questioned Risa, "What do you think?"

"Perhaps we should ask Carlos."

When no one objected, Risa said, "I'll ask him to join us."

They welcomed Carlos and then explained their desire to better understand his Circle.

"We come to the Circle with open hearts, linked to every other heart," he said. "We listen. When we Hear —peace flows within each of us. One spokesperson will speak the message. We go forth together."

Gemma asked, "Who is the spokesperson?"

"Anyone—each of us—whoever Hears what comes from the Circle."

Each of them thought about that.

Carlos explained: "We left our home in the West at the direction of our Circle. We Knew without knowing to come here—a place we knew nothing about."

Risa muttered, "That's about as cryptic as ours."

Lilla said, "So, we should all stay here."

Carlos responded, "That is true for us. It may not be true for you."

Brit said, "Yes. Exactly. We must become open to our own Circle of Intent." She paused a moment. "I think there may be many Circles throughout the world that we may meet."

Echoing her, Gemma added, "We must deepen our commitment to our Circle. And we must trust The Shift."

Carlos gave a slight nod, "Yes. I think so." He then rose, bowed to the group, and walked away.

Misha said, "Let's focus on our Intent in this

evening's Circle. We will know what is next for us."

"Sure," said Gemma, laughing. "And let's see if we can do that without 'doing' anything." She appreciated their smiles.

That evening their toning easily fell into harmony and then into the silence that followed. As their breath became one, an ease permeated the group. Their energies flowed and became intertwined.

'Survive to Serve' became the unspoken focus for each woman as images appeared in each of their minds: women on horseback, cloaks of different colors flowing behind them as they cantered effortlessly together, their heads held high, their bodies erect and full of purpose.

One by one, their eyes opened as the visions faded. Deeper breaths were taken in and then released.

They Knew. Preparations for leaving was their next step.

Lilla and Risa packed each duffel to be loaded onto the horses.

"But what about the gangs?" Lilla was anxious and was pushing Risa to unite with her.

Risa kept packing as Lilla pestered her for a

response.

Finally, Risa stopped and faced her. "You saw it too, right?"

Lilla slumped. "Yes. I had a vision. So what? That doesn't change the reality of what we will face!" She grew more excited now that she had Risa's attention. "We are *safe here!*"

Risa had had enough. "Lilla, you are welcome to stay here as long as you wish. Or you can take your horse and head North and go home." She snapped hard at the ties.

"Not alone!"

"Finally. You get it." She put her hands on Lilla's arms. "Together, we are strong. I believe we even have power—together. If you don't believe that, then stay—or leave—but our unity is essential." She dropped her hold on Lilla but looked into her eyes. "I hope you will have the courage to leave the group if you can't unite with the intent."

Lilla's mouth dropped open. She didn't know what to say.

Risa grabbed Lilla's shoulders and gave her a shake. "Wake up, Lilla! Don't let fear take over."

Lilla sniffed, shaken at this new Risa.

"OK, OK," she said. "I just needed to…"

"Vent?" Risa finished for her.

Lilla nodded.

"That doesn't help at this point," Risa said as she hugged her. "Come on. Let's get the packing done."

* * *

Carlos and his young men sped up the group's training in caring for their horses and teaching special riding techniques they might need.

Misha insisted they enhance their focus on their Intent each evening.

Risa thanked the women in the kitchen who were preparing food that would last them on their journey. Their knowledge about drying the ripe fruits from the orchard and vegetables from the garden was invaluable. Nuts and seeds were packaged from the emergency storeroom. Jerky had been prepared earlier and was added to their supplies.

Brit and Gemma were studying the map Risa had found for them. There was no way to know which path was blocked or where they might encounter gangs that Carlos' man had seen or heard about.

Gemma tried to encourage Brit. "We have to start somewhere."

Brit patted Gem's arm as they studied the map. "You're right, of course. And we have to be flexible enough to change directions if we must."

"How do you think the others are doing?" Gem asked her.

"Risa amazes me. It's not just her expertise. It's her attitude and desire to take care of others."

"I agree. I underestimated her. She'll bring Lilla around."

"I hope so. She is the only one who can."

* * *

Carlos supervised the loading of supplies onto the horses. At the same time, he whispered instructions, reassurances, as well as his own energy into the ears of each horse.

As the women's departure came closer, he drew two of his men aside. He gave them the mission to follow the women without being seen by them, and to map mentally the open paths South. He emphasized that protection was their primary mission.

Carlos had brought his people together into their Circle the previous night. Their focus was protection for the women on their journey, and protection for their own home here.

The energy intensified, swirling and spinning outward, encircling the women and Carlos' people. After their ceremony, each held the intention in their hearts.

CHAPTER 17

The first few hours of riding got the women used to being on horseback for extended periods. The main roads were full of boulders that had shaken loose from the mountainsides. Only animal trails were still passable in many places.

Alert at first, the rhythmic clop of horses hooves began to lull them into a relaxed state. The path gradually sloped upward along the side of the mountain. They could spy the ranch house in the far off distance until the path curved and erased the view of Risa's ranch.

The sunny day, cooled with the still gentle spring breezes, lifted their spirits. Brit and Gemma had plotted their path and chosen a likely camping spot for the end of their first day. They reached the designated campsite by early afternoon. They were more than ready to dismount and move their tired limbs and stretch out the kinks.

Risa supervised each one's care of her horse. She watched as they inspected their hooves for any stones embedded and then removed them.

Misha slowly walked around the perimeter of the site, and when she returned to the starting point, she acknowledged that energetically this was a good spot. Brit thanked her and glanced at Gem, knowing that she would be annoyed at needing Misha's approval.

Risa gathered stones for a fire pit. Lilla went off to find firewood as Brit and Gem selected the best area to bed down. Supplies for their dinner were unloaded.

They had stopped early enough to allow for how long it took them this first day to set up a camp. However, it was still close to evening by the time they finished their first meal on the road.

Once they cleared the area, they gathered for the evening Circle. After so many evening Circles, the hum began spontaneously, with each one effortlessly finding a harmonious tone as she joined. This night a soprano descant wove in and out of their song-without-words, ethereal, mystical.

They completed the day at peace within and with each other. Sleep came quickly.

The horses gave the first warning with snorting and stamping, startling the women awake. The fire had almost burned itself out, leaving only glowing coals to see by.

Brit unrolled herself from her warm cloak made into a bed. With her flashlight, she walked quietly around the perimeter. As she approached the horses, they quieted, seemingly reassured by her presence.

When she returned to her spot next to an alert Gemma, she said, "I think we had better post sentries at night. Two-hour shifts will still give each of us enough sleep."

Gemma agreed, and she began to get up until Brit stopped her, and said, "I think we are OK now. Whatever spooked the horses seems to have backed off. They have settled down."

Gemma reluctantly lay back on her cloak. "Nevertheless, I'll keep watch from here."

The next two nights passed without incident. Each woman took a shift, watching and listening for any disturbances.

They had settled into an efficient rhythm: up at

daybreak, a nutrition pack for breakfast, break camp, and erase any signs of their presence. Feed, then load the horses and begin again along the narrow path.

They had been able to see from their trail high on the mountainside the devastation below them. No one would be driving on the destroyed highway for a long time… if ever.

Once in awhile, they spotted carrion birds high overhead, circling. Whether an animal or human remains attracted them, they didn't stop to investigate.

Early on the third day, they found a small meadow that was perfect for their horses. They could graze their fill. The trickling stream was especially welcome. Finding water had become an ongoing concern.

Lilla volunteered to search for firewood as each of them set about, what by now, were familiar tasks. Their friendly bantering created a harmony of its own. Suddenly, their peace was suddenly shattered by a piercing scream.

LILLA!

Without thought, frozen where they were, spontaneously, they began an open-throated sound that reverberated and echoed off the slabs of rock that encircled the campsite. Not a scream nor a yell, but an escalating discordant call that culminated in an urgent, focused, high-pitched, piercing sound directed toward where they had last seen Lilla.

It stopped abruptly as Lilla appeared, running toward them. They ran to her, embracing her as she fell into their arms.

Misha disengaged from the group embrace. *What had happened? To Lilla—to them?* She signaled that they should move into their Circle. She began the hum, low-pitched, soothing. Each found another's hand until the Circle was complete.

"We have power. Unknown power," said Misha in her quiet voice. "It matters. We must harness this power, not only for our own protection but for those we are sent to protect."

Brit added, "Yes—in service to others."

In her practical way, Gemma said, "We, from now on, will do things in twos. No one should be alone outside the camp."

Brit reminded everyone that they were able to protect Lilla, even when she was out of their sight.

They turned to Lilla, who was huddled close to Risa. She encouraged Lilla to tell them what had happened.

In a subdued voice, she told them, "I was gathering

firewood, just out of sight of the rest of you. I felt uneasy, but shrugged it off to being paranoid. Then I saw the spring down below me. I thought we might have a chance to bathe. I started down to investigate when someone grabbed me from behind and tried to drag me away.

"I was so shocked. I screamed—and then your sound echoed all around me. I joined you! Somehow. Whoever it was panicked and fled, letting me go. And then I ran back to all of you."

Risa, with her arm around Lilla, could feel her shaking. "But we did it! You—all of us—are safe!"

Brit sitting, head balanced on her knees considering said, "I'm not sure 'safe' is the word." She looked at each of them. "Perhaps this was a warning."

"Of what?" asked Gem.

"I don't know. But I think… I feel… we must accept that danger is around us. We must be prepared." Brit turned her attention to Misha. "Tell us what you Know or Hear."

Misha took in a deep breath held it, and then slowly released it. "We have power, especially together. We released sound today that frightened an enemy away."

"Yes!" said Lilla, still panicky. "But what if there are more of them, a gang…"

"Exactly," said Misha. "*We do have the power to repel evil intent. But do we have the power to inspire?*"

Brit answered, "I think I understand. It isn't enough to scare off people. We must create an energy that attracts that people want to join."

Risa said, "Just how, exactly, do we do that?"

"Misha must help us find that power," Brit said. "Our experience today showed us our power to protect. The positive element will also reveal itself."

CHAPTER 18

"Where's Carlos? I have to find Carlos!" yelled the boy even before dismounting. He threw the reins to the young men who pointed him toward the house, and he ran full speed in that direction.

As he neared the house, he saw Carlos talking with Carmella on the veranda.

"Carlos! I must speak with you," he said, trying hard to control his heaving chest.

Carlos beckoned the agitated lad onto the veranda. This was one of the young men he had sent to oversee the safety of the women.

"Calm yourself. Catch your breath and then tell me what is so urgent."

"A banshee! The sound of the banshee!" he cried as he collapsed into a chair.

Carlos became very still. He waited for the boy to

collect himself.

Finally, the boy spoke. In a somewhat rambling fashion, he reported that Lilla had been captured, and the women had set her free—with the cry of the banshee.

At Carlos' urging, he tried to describe the sound he had heard, but he became more and more agitated. Carlos placed a gentle hand on his back until the young man calmed. He spoke to him in soothing tones and then sent him to go with Carmella for food and drink.

Carlos sat, musing over this news. The women protected themselves. They unleashed their united power. He smiled, then nodded. A huge sigh escaped him. *They can now take care of themselves.*

Carlos pulled himself into his stillness and focused on his message to the lad's companion, who was still far off, watching the women.

"Come home. Your mission is completed." Then he waited.

Soon he Heard the response, *"I come."*

Carlos went into the house, satisfied. For now, all were safe.

* * *

Misha rode her horse with ease, happy to be traveling toward their goal—to serve others.

Although she was concerned about Lilla's narrow escape, she was thrilled at what impelled them to create that extraordinary sound. Her confidence in the Circle was boundless. She Knew they could do anything as long as they kept faith with the Circle of Intent.

The narrow path kept them riding one behind the other in a long line, inhibiting conversation. Each was lost in her own thoughts and feelings about the previous night.

Brit could sense the jumbled emotions of the group. Hers were not different. The eerie sound that emanated from them into one voice like a laser beam had saved Lilla. Where had it come from? She fell into Diablo's clop, clop rhythm, and just let her feelings of amazement, fear, and then comfort, wash over her. Her confidence in their mission was growing.

Gemma wasn't content to simply appreciate the power that was being revealed to them. *What more can we do*, still occupied her mind.

Risa was proud of her horses, of their awareness and their warnings of danger. She realized that her pride was in them, not herself. She chuckled softly as she rode. Maybe Lilla would stop her complaining now. Surely her confidence in their Circle had to grow.

Lilla found herself deep in thought about the whole incident. Had her fears about this journey attracted... *No. Surely not. That was silly, even spooky.* She tried to shut that feeling off.

Still... The teachings from her years in The Gathering were surfacing lately, especially during their ceremonies. She didn't *want* to be responsible for everything that happened to her. She tried to discount the idea she could attract bad things into her life. Apparently, not too successfully.

In her own mind, she had ridiculed Misha, with her 'Circle' this and 'Circle' that. Difficult to do that now. Everyone had begun talking about their power— together. Could it be true? Even real?

She found herself wanting to believe it was real. She was so tired of feeling afraid. That thought startled her. She was afraid, almost all the time, like a habit she couldn't break, or even want to break.

Hope. Did she dare to hope? Hope that she could give up being afraid? The thought sent shivers up her spine. She sat up higher on her horse.

* * *

They chose the next campsite carefully. Risa emphasized that sentries should not only watch but listen for any restlessness from the horses as well.

Their usual tasks were completed quickly. All were eager to gather for their ceremony. Brit, however, wanted first to investigate areas around the site for possible hiding places from which an attack could come. She also made it clear that no one was to go alone anywhere for any reason.

They agreed although Gemma brought up their hope of bathing in a stream close by. They felt the need as well as the desire to become clean after their days in the saddle.

Brit acquiesced as long as four women were watching as one by one each bathed. "It seems safe enough," she said, turning toward them—but they had quickly already left to prepare.

CHAPTER 19

Brit pulled her snug, green cloak around her against the increasingly cold night air. As tired as she was, it was difficult to fall asleep. As she began to drift off, the image of Noah appeared. She lay very still, not wanting it to disappear.

"Come to the Gathering's place. I'm waiting for you." His smile flooded her heart. He reached an arm toward her, beckoning her to take his hand and come with him.

Brit tried to move, to sit up so she could touch him before his image faded. As it disappeared, tears coursed down her face. Finally, sleep rescued her.

At dawn, Brit woke, somehow reassured that Noah was alive and was waiting for them. Her cheerful low whistle as they set about clearing the campsite brought smiles to everyone.

Gem asked, "A dream, Brit?"

Brit just smiled back, aware that they all knew. She realized she wasn't disturbed by their knowing. Lack of privacy no longer seemed to matter. Rather, she appreciated the love she experienced—that she could feel coming from them.

Amazing, she thought. Then she resumed her comfortable, if unmelodious, whistling as she went about her tasks.

One more day would take them out of the mountains to the edge of the desert. Gemma was very aware that they needed to plan how to best traverse the looming desert ahead.

As she rode, she contemplated how long it would take them to cross the vast expanse by horseback. Traveling at night would slow them down, but the heat during the day could be more of an obstacle. She was grateful that there would be a full moon in a couple of nights. They needed to be ready by then. She and Brit needed to have a powwow tonight.

They needed to choose the next campsite with the horses their priority. They had to be well fed and watered before starting across the desert.

Their travel had become almost routine. Questions that Gemma had repressed began popping into her mind as they got closer to towns and more roads. What conditions would the quakes have left? Would there be people? Would they be friendly or hostile? Would they be able to replenish any of their supplies? What lies ahead of us?

The refugees who had made it to Risa's had made it sound horrendous. But then she tried to reassure herself, *people tend to exaggerate in order to impress. Well, we will know when we get there.*

In the morning, Gemma and Brit huddled together over their map one more time, deciding the best route across the desert.

As Lilla and Misha worked together clearing the campsite, Risa took off to retrieve the horses grazing in the nearby meadow. Gemma decided to follow her— just to be safe.

Sunshine responded first to Risa's call. Diablo and Ginger quickly followed her lead. Misha's Cloud followed Blaze only after a stern reminder from Risa. She laughed to herself as she realized that, once again, she was indebted to her palomino for somehow keeping the other horses in line.

The chilly, spring morning air had everyone moving swiftly.

Tasks completed, they came together to discuss the next portion of their journey. Gemma pointed out the route. Brit let them know they would travel at night to avoid heat.

Today they would find a site near the edge of the desert and then rest until evening, when they would begin their trek.

The uncertainty of what was ahead subdued their usual morning chatter. Without comments, they mounted their horses and headed into unknown territory.

The women reached the edge of the desert just as white flakes began falling from dark, glowering clouds. They established their camp in a protected area under a large flat rock overhang. With a fire made, they shook off the cold. A late spring snow! Not exactly the heat they anticipated.

They were concerned. They needed clear skies and the full moon to continue across the desert. Wind had also come up, sending howling echoes throughout their hideaway. Their gloom matched the dark day.

"Okay, it's a day of rest," said Lilla. "I, for one, am ready for that."

The others laughed in agreement, shaking off their bleak mood.

Risa said, "I think I could sleep for the whole day."

Brit gave in to their 'Let's make lemonade out of these lemons' attitude. "Me too," she said. "My old bones welcome a day of rest." She looked at Misha. "How do you feel, Misha?"

"We *could* do an extended Circle," Misha said.

To their groaned response, she gave a big smile. "Just a thought."

Gemma piped up, "Some things are funny. *That* was not!" More laughter greeted her.

"We do need to make sure the horses are protected," Risa said as she rose and headed to the entrance of their enclave.

"I'll help," Lilla said and followed her out.

"Good," Gem said. "Nobody goes alone."

Brit spoke to Gem, "Do you think we need sentries tonight?"

Gem nodded. "We can't afford to relax our vigilance. We don't know who or what may come our way." She looked at Brit's drooping body, huddled close to the fire. "I'll take the first shift. You go lie down and get some rest." To Brit's beginning objection, she said, "You are no good to us if you are exhausted."

Gratefully, Brit snuggled into her cloak and little by little relaxed her stiff muscles into sleep.

* * *

After two days, the spring snowstorm dribbled out, leaving a white expanse as far as they could see. As the sun rose higher, the sound of dripping melting snow filled the air.

They left at dawn, trying to make up the time they had lost waiting out the snowstorm. By noon, the wet snow had disappeared, making their progress less tentative.

"Well, this is different," said Lilla as they made their way slowly.

Risa's concern was for the safety of the horses. She took the lead, staying on the bare ground where the snow had melted. They moved slowly but made progress through the day.

Each day followed the next, making this part of their

journey tedious. The unusually hot sun had quickly baked the earth, turning mud into dust, erasing all traces of the snowstorm. They rode, taking only brief rest stops until darkness made travel too dangerous.

A few days later, as they rode across the seemingly endless desert, in the distance, they saw what appeared to be a gigantic dirt-gray cloud rising up from the ground, towering so high it blocked the distant views of the mountains. It was moving toward them. Risa shouted out, "Habub!" Her urgency stopped them.

Misha took over, "Come, fast!" The women slipped down to cover their horses' eyes with their scarves. Quickly, they then formed a Circle, spreading their cloaks wide. Each woman caught hold of the edges of the cloaks next to them. The cloaks, seemingly without effort, billowed up their rainbow colors into a tent. As their hoods covered their faces, they began to hum in unison.

The dust and ferocious winds roared over them. They hummed and huddled against the dust storm for what seemed like hours. As the horrendous noise faded away, they sank to the ground, stunned. At last, they moved. They shook the dust off their cloaks as they approached their horses, who had not moved. They carefully removed the blindfolds. Their horses had withstood the ordeal. All was well.

The dust storm had happened so quickly, they had no time to think, let alone prepare. They just acted. Their cloaks had been a refuge that protected them. That the horses had known to stand close together in a pack surprised even Risa.

No one seemed to want to talk about what had happened. It was clear: their mission, their intention was their protection.

Their Circle that night was filled with deep feelings of gratitude.

Traveling the next day, the mountain range ahead still seemed impossibly far off. The one positive element was the dry air and the gentle feel of the warm sun as they road. As their spirits rose, Misha began a hum. One by one, they joined her, letting the vibrations embrace them.

By evening they had made their way through a good half of the desert before them. As the sky darkened, Gemma noticed specks of light far off in different parts of the mountain. "Fires," she noted, pointing them out to the others.

They decided to rest, eat a meal, and after their Circle

continue on under a full moon that would finally light their way.

For the first time, they would meet other travelers, people heading North, escaping what?

Riding through most of the night, they stopped before heading into the pass.

The evening's Circle began with a softer hum, their energy subdued but still flowing through them. No one spoke aloud, yet they sensed each other's concerns, as well as their commitment to one another.

They were very ready to bed down for what remained of the night. Sleep was needed.

CHAPTER 20

Although their rest had been minimal, they were more than ready to move as the sun rose.

Gemma's concerns about the fires and what they might indicate were everyone's concerns. As they tuned into each other, the urgency to investigate what was ahead took hold.

Risa rode up beside Brit and Gemma. "I should go on ahead and check out the situation we may face."

Brit negated the idea. "Our protection is together. No one alone, remember?"

Gem said to them, "True, but we need to know."

Misha tuned in, "We need to present ourselves as a force with the intention to help, not hurt."

They rode in silence, mulling over how they might accomplish this. Once again, it became clear that their best answers and direction came through their Circle.

When they came upon an oasis near the edge of the desert, their relief was palpable. That many had been there before them was obvious from the many animal tracks. They silently agreed that they needed to stop here, rest, and prepare for the next part of their journey through the mountain pass.

They made camp, and although it was early afternoon, not sunset, as One, they went into their Circle, began their hum simultaneously, growing into a full-throated song-without-words. As it diminished and faded into silence, they soundlessly sank down onto the sand.

At last, Misha spoke, "We must always present as One. That is our protection. Also, it will allow us to serve wherever needed. The word will spread about us —that we are women who serve, and must be allowed to pass; no harm or hindrance will block our way.

"Our intention must be manifested through our service. It must be at the forefront of each mind—but as One.

"Do we so vow?"

They answered as One: "Yes, we survive to serve."

The women disbursed and set about personal tasks, preparing for a very different terrain than the desert they had finally left behind.

A small pool was discovered, and they took turns bathing and watching for any intruders.

They each were very conscientious about caring for the needs of their horses. Finding water and a place for them to graze came before preparing their own food. The women had come to realize that The Shift had definitely enhanced the intelligence of their animals. They always seemed to know the best paths and safest routes to take without direction. They also seemed to be able to communicate with each other as well as with their riders.

There was less chatter among the women. Their enhanced ability to Know had increased with each major challenge they had faced together. They didn't discuss it. It just was. There was a peace in Knowing, and they embraced it.

Refreshed by their half-day and night of rest, they rose the next morning, and as one, they reversed their cloaks. The sienna color of the inner material merged with the sand and rocks and boulders of the mountains.

Silently, they re-mounted their horses and began making their way through the mountain pass.

They rode through several small encampments, riding

most of the day. No one approached them or even called out to the women. Their united presence spoke for them.

A stream ran through the bottom of the pass, and they made camp near it, relishing the quiet sound of the trickling water as they wrapped themselves in their cloaks and slept.

Risa heard the neighing of horses, not their own. She quickly roused the others. Taking their cloaks, they gathered silently into a tight circle. They waited.

Hooves clanged on the flat rocks as the strangers approached. They stopped close by. No one from the group spoke.

Finally, a man's deep voice broke the tense silence. "Are you the women we have heard about?"

"What have you heard?" Gemma's voice carried with authority to the men.

"We hear that women on horses are going through the pass. Alone."

"We are not alone." They spoke as One.

Another voice called out, "We mean no harm. We are willing to help." A young voice.

Brit raised her head and called out. "Your offer to

help is appreciated, but not needed. However, you may, if you wish, do us a service."

The first man spoke, "Tell us. We will do what we can."

"Let all others know we move as One. Our objective is to serve where wanted or needed. We will do no harm to those whose intentions are for the higher good."

"We can do that, ma'am." They turned their horses and rode away.

The women went to their horses, loaded their packs, and set out once again just as dawn's light made traveling safe for their horses. No one spoke. Lost in their thoughts, the time went quickly. Finally, they stopped for a mid-day meal, everyone hungry after missing breakfast.

Once everyone was supplied with coffee and a nutrition pack, Misha spoke to her sisters. "I think we know our mission is blessed, and that we are and will be protected as long as our intention stays clear."

Lilla spoke up, "I would like to know what happened! How did we do that?"

Brit answered, "I don't think any of us Know."

Gemma continued Brit's thought, "Isn't it enough

that we have seen the evidence? We are protected. Period."

Risa spoke up, "I still think we should continue with sentries. If I hadn't heard their horses neighing, we don't know what the strangers might have intended."

Misha said, "Yes, vigilance is necessary."

Brit said, "All right. We shall do our part, appreciating the protection of the Circle, but not taking it for granted. Are we agreed?"

They indicated an agreement.

The following days passed peacefully. At times they met other travelers, most going North. They listened to their stories, offered a peaceful place to rest before the strangers continued their trek. This slowed their own progress through the pass but increased their sense of mission.

Others were curious about five women traveling alone through what they had experienced as dangerous territory. The women mainly listened, not offering solutions or advice. Yet the travelers experienced the peace and confidence these women exuded. Travelers left with more confidence and resilience.

More and more often, people said they had heard

about the five women traveling alone through the pass with seemingly magical powers. Whether hesitant or assertive, they were intensely curious. Some wanted to join them but were told that was not possible. Gemma was the one who made it clear that stories of magic were just that, stories.

The women were increasingly eager to get to the end of the pass through the mountains. They were told by others that just beyond the mountains, they would reach the ocean. They could hardly wait.

CHAPTER 21

Noah's sun-streaked hair glinted beneath the bright sun. His broad sweaty back was already sunburned. His shirt had come off hours ago. Building a basic shelter for the survivors was backbreaking work.

The work kept everyone going forward, instead of wallowing in self-pity or despair. *Men and women together worked to—what?* he wondered. *Pretending that there was a normal they were working toward?*

Noah reminded himself that it didn't matter what anyone thought. Survival meant more than food and shelter. The spirit had to thrive if any of it made any sense.

The large beam was ready to be set in the center of the building they were constructing. It would take all of them to lift and then stabilize it. It would be the main support for the building—a fancy word for the structure. But it would suffice for awhile—a shelter for a few souls. He moved forward to add his weight to the effort.

As he leaned in against the beam, his thoughts went to Brit. Where was she, he wondered? How had she managed after he left? The responsibility weighed on him, that is, when he had energy left at the end of the day.

He caught snippets of energy from her at times, especially when he was just drifting into sleep. Whatever that was about. They had been so distant from one another.

He'd found survivors all right—he had just never imagined the devastation caused by the mega-quake. Their LA home was gone, not damaged, demolished. So he had headed to the place near the beach that The Gathering had occupied. Lucky to be almost on the beach. More incredible was that anything was left after the powerful waves of the tsunami had swept in.

It was possible to get clean—if a little salty—in the ocean, once most of the debris from the tsunami had by now floated out to sea.

One more effort by everyone to straighten the beam, and it was in place. That was enough for the day. He found a towel to wipe himself down.

Still thinking about Brit, somehow he didn't visualize her alone, although he didn't know who else might be there with her. The dome had been his inspired idea. He did, indeed, like being validated!

The day's work done, everyone pitched in to set up for their communal supper. The government had set up 'soup kitchens.' Food and other supplies were helicoptered into key sites throughout the city. Volunteers trudged out every day to bring back whatever was available to feed and supply the workers.

Hygiene had been an issue at first. It was better now. Thanks to Jake. He was a wonder at getting the important things done.

Noah and Jake had become fast friends soon after Noah arrived in the destroyed city. Noah had holed up in one of the improvised shelters after discovering that their home had been obliterated by the quake.

When Jake came into the soup-kitchen with the food and other supplies for the survivors, Noah had offered to help Jake unload. It was strange, but Noah felt he knew Jake from somewhere. They ended up chatting over their improvised supper.

"I was in the city during the quake," Jake told him.

"Most people were struggling to leave the city, but I decided to stay and help wherever I could."

Jake was strong, fit in his thirties, and alone. "I had no trouble finding work," he laughed.

Noah didn't doubt that Jake would be welcomed wherever he went. His upbeat optimism and a broad smile lit up his dark, handsome face.

Noah told him his plan: to find survivors of The Gathering, a group he had been with before building his real home up North.

Jake smiled, then looked down at his supper.

"What?" Noah asked.

"I thought that was you," Jake said. "I hung around that group for a little while—checking out the women, mostly." He looked up at Noah. "I'm surprised you would..." He shrugged his question.

Noah didn't quite know how to respond.

"I'm curious that you would have been part of such a group," Jake said. "I left because the Gathering felt like a cult to me."

Noah laughed when Jake confessed they had tried to recruit him. "Yes, I am sure they would have been very happy to have you join them."

Noah told him, "The group actually was like a small community. There were some awesome people, and then there were others. After the Big One, I worried about them. They had a place near the ocean where everyone used to gather. So I've come to LA to see if anyone had ended up there. Help them if I could." Noah could see that Jake was interested. "I'm on my way there now. Want to come?"

Jake gathered up his stuff and said, "Let's go!"

Noah got his things together and confessed, "I have no idea what to expect."

"I guess we'll find out. Lead the way."

Noah quickly scoped out the camp, hoping to find anybody from The Gathering. There were none. He was disappointed, but when he saw how much work was needed to finish the structure, he and Jake offered to lend a hand. They were enthusiastically welcomed.

They got to know one another as they worked side by side with a hammer and saw. The old building was gone. However, a semi-new structure was being built. People were salvaging pieces left on the beach by the tsunami. It was just a temporary structure, but it would house a few dozen people.

As Jake got to know Noah, he was curious about his story. He wasn't hesitant about asking what would have led him to join a group such as The Gathering.

"Yeah, I know it seems unlikely," Noah said. "I'm a boy from a typical, conservative family—two parents and an older sister, Carrie. We even had a dog named Molly." He paused. "Carrie was killed in a car crash. That changed everything."

"Oh, man, I'm sorry," Jake said.

"She was older than I—pretty, smart, and a little wild —got in with a bad crowd."

"Where did you go from there?" Jake asked.

"College—communication major as well as business, to please the parents." He shrugged as he bent to his work on the plank he was planing. "A scholarship was offered. So I went."

"I'm going to guess," Jake said as he checked out Noah's broad-shouldered, trim physique, "that you were a swimmer."

Noah nodded. "Yeah, for as long as I lasted. It seemed pretty meaningless after Carrie was gone. I left."

"So, when did you find the Gathering?"

"I stumbled into it actually—at a bar of all places. This guy came up to me. We started talking. It was probably obvious to him what condition I was in. Anyway, he invited me to check out this group he belonged to."

"So, you went?"

"It was actually pretty positive. I certainly needed an alternative to the negative mess I was falling into. And at first, it was an incredible relief to be with all these positive people. I didn't pay much attention to the Elders, as they were called. That is until they started paying more attention to me. They were into recruiting, and I fit their type to bring in the ladies: tall, blond, blue-eyed—athletic."

"Oh yeah. And you bought it?"

"Not really—until I met Brit. She was lovely, fragile, although very intense about helping others find their path or their truth, as she called it. We would end up talking most of the night. At some point, our relationship became more intimate... We became a couple. She was pretty high up in their hierarchy, and the Elders began pushing us to marry. I think both of us were hesitant, but we went ahead and had a small ceremony. Her parents, as well as mine, were gone, and the community had become everything to her."

"Where is—Brit? That her name?"

"She's up North in the dome house that I built before the Big One hit." He gave a bitter laugh. "You know, it was wonderful until the Elders butt their noses into our lives. I knew in my gut that there was more meaning to life than what they were espousing. 'Get more people; get them to contribute; etc., etc.' Somehow, she clung to her ideals, ignoring their increasing dictates. She genuinely wanted to help people 'find their truth,' as she expressed it.

"Then, the mini-quakes started happening. I thought, or hoped, she was starting to wake up. But we seemed to drift further apart." Noah put down the hammer that he was wielding.

"I became obsessed with architecture that could withstand earthquakes and extreme weather conditions. The dome became the obvious choice. I had land up North my parents willed to me years ago as well as money to build. And I did!

"Brit thought it a crazy idea. She couldn't understand my motive for leaving her and building so far away. She winced at my dismissal of the Gathering, which created a huge rift in our relationship. I left. We stayed in contact, and I even communicated with the Elders from time to time at her urging. They were becoming fearful as the mini-quakes increased in frequency and magnitude. Brit finally began questioning them about the direction the Gathering was taking. She got no answers from them that satisfied. She stopped even trying to talk to me.

"I began to worry when weeks went by without any contact. I knew I had to go South to LA and try to convince Brit to come up North and see for herself what I had built. I just knew she would be astounded at the design and functionality of the dome."

Noah wiped the sweat from his brow as he shook his head in disbelief at the memory. He choked back a sob and then took in a big breath. "When I found her, she was nearly unconscious, curled in our bed, dehydrated, her forehead clammy. As soon as she could travel, I took her up North."

His hammer pounded the nails into the wood, expressing better than his words, the guilt he felt.

"And then the Big One hit. Her beliefs and confidence in the Elders shattered along with everything around us—except for the dome. She was at a loss, more than I realized. She was isolated from her community and certainly from me, her husband. I couldn't understand her stubborn unwillingness to recognize that the Gathering was a sham and hurt the followers. She withdrew more and more, I took it very personally. That didn't help at all. I tried to convince her and myself that I was truly concerned about the fate of the group in LA. And in spite of Brit's passivity, which I interpreted as hostility, I left. I was determined to find survivors—if I could." He looked at Jake, shrugged, and then said, "No such luck."

"She is still there?" asked Jake.

"As far as I know," Noah admitted, silenced and somewhat shamefaced. Both of them bent to their work.

Noah had found solace in being with the volunteers. He was encouraged as he saw that people with a goal somehow found a way to organize and get things done. Admirable really.

At day's end, he found his corner where he'd left his blanket bedroll. He was too tired to notice any discomfort. He slept. No dreams tonight.

CHAPTER 22

Horses hooves pounded the sand in rhythm with each other, to the delight of the women. Their multi-hued cloaks billowed behind them, lending credence to onlookers' visions that they were almost flying.

Their relief at being out of the desert and mountains expressed itself in joyous laughter as they cantered onto the wet sand, slowing finally to take a long look at the ocean. It was only as they had slowed to a walk that they took note of the destruction they could see as they looked inland.

It was hard to take in what looked like a war zone. The amount of total demolition was beyond what they had imagined they would see. It sobered them quickly. Even after three years, people were living in tents here and there along the beachfront. Apparently, after the tsunami had hit, people still retreated toward the ocean in their panic.

Without an actual destination, they decided to camp in one of the coves along the beach, away from others' tents. They needed to collect themselves as well as rest after their arduous journey through desert and mountains. One by one, each bathed in the ocean while the others stood watch. It was difficult to want to stay alert, their relief at reaching some sort of destination was so palpable.

Risa made sure the stream coming out of the pass provided fresh water for the horses. Each agreed that a sentry was wise, and they would each take a turn. Sleep overcame them quickly, and nothing that night disturbed their rest.

* * *

"Hey, Noah!" Jake, who was running toward him, yelled.

Noah, just getting out of his bed, turned around, "Hey, Jake, what's up?"

Out of breath, Jake said, "All the guys up the way have sighted a group of horsemen galloping along the beach. They're coming this way."

"Dangerous?"

"No one knows. Not yet, anyway."

"Well, we better go meet them," Noah said. He threw on his pants and a t-shirt and followed Jake. Neither minded being late to their work crew. In the distance, they spotted horses and riders coming toward them.

"Those are *women*," Jake shouted enthusiastically to Noah as they strode along at the edge of the water toward them.

Noah laughed at his dark, curly-haired friend. But just as he was about to tease this self-styled macho guy, he stopped cold. He looked again. "Who—?" Noah was dumbfounded as he realized that one of the riders was his wife.

The women slowed, then reined in their steeds and stopped in front of the men who gaped at their arrival. Brit slid off Diablo and rushed to embrace Noah. He held her close before he set her on her feet.

"You came," he said. "You *all* came."

Brit exclaimed, "We did! I Heard your call, your message."

Noah's face showed his puzzlement. He pulled away from Brit, putting distance between them.

Brit paused, waiting. But when there was no acknowledgment from him, she said, "We'll talk later,

OK?" She turned back to her sisters, who had also dismounted. "Where shall we camp tonight, Ladies?" she asked.

Gemma stepped up beside her, gave Noah a brief nod, and said to Brit, "I saw a small cove a short distance away that we passed. I think it should do until we find more suitable quarters." She gave a final look at Noah.

Brit nodded her acceptance and gave a quizzical look at Noah. "Let me know when you are free," she said as she mounted once again.

"Hope to meet you," she called to Jake as they sped off, following Gem toward the aforementioned cove.

Jake looked away from the women to face Noah, "I know that lady!

"Who?"

"The blond one on the palomino."

"Are you sure?" Noah asked.

"Oh yeah. And I know she wants nothing to do with me!"

"Well, I'll be damned," answered Noah, too blown away by Brit's arrival to pay much attention to what Jake was telling him. He bowed his head, thinking about his intense dreams. *Had they reached their target? Was it possible that Brit's feelings had changed?* He didn't know whether to be pleased or unhappy. What did he want? Could their relationship be repaired?

He shook his head and turned to Jake, "Come on, let's get started on the project."

"Mighty fine, handsome women," Jake offered, needling Noah just a little.

"Yeah, yeah," said Noah as he stalked off.

Brit asked Gemma as she rode up beside her, "Where is this cove?"

"I've no idea," Gem answered. "I wasn't about to let you ask Noah where we can stay."

Brit gave her a quick smile. She understood that Gem had read the situation accurately.

Riding slowly, they saw several possible sites that could meet their needs. Brit rode her horse with back straight, head held high, letting Gem and the others do the looking for the best campsite.

What had she expected? They hadn't parted exactly amicably. Had she put too much faith in the Circle? She felt his pull so intensely. Was that just imagination or worse, wish-fulfillment?

What *did* she want? Then she remembered: to serve.

Survive to Serve. Warmth filled her body. She relaxed into the gentle, rhythmic movements of Diablo.

* * *

Noah was conflicted as he threw himself into the construction work. Why had she come? *Had* he sent a message? He knew a part of him had missed her—or what they once had meant to each other.

And what were those other women doing with her? He spat in disgust. Nothing but trouble, those four. His hammer took several powerful hits before he paused.

He couldn't erase that image of the five, racing down the beach on those beautiful animals. They seemed so in sync with each other. Their colorful cloaks or capes they wore—billowing behind them, almost as if they could leave earth and fly away.

He shook his head in wonderment as he took up the hammer again. It seemed with every hit, a new question arose. *Where can they stay?* Then he reminded himself that they didn't seem to need any help from him. *Did she come to bring him back? To get him to go North?*

He was happy here, helping the people who had survived. Interesting that no Elders had shown up here.

A few of the Gatherers had come. But when they saw the destruction, they left again.

His dreams had been intense at times, especially about Brit, but he had no sense of sending her messages.

His hammer expressed his frustrations. *What are these four women doing with Brit? They certainly were no friends of hers in the past, no matter what she thought.* His own history with these particular women wasn't particularly good. *And what was Misha doing hanging out with Lilla? No love lost between those two. And what was Risa doing with these women? Why was she away from her ranch?* He guessed that was where they got the horses.

He stopped his hammering as another thought struck him: he had never seen Brit on a horse before—and she was so confident. *What had happened?*

He could see that Jake was very curious about Noah's connection to the women. He wasn't sure what he would tell him.

"Hey, Noah," Jake called, trying to catch his attention, midst all the din from the hammering and sawing around them. "Noah," he shouted, finally getting his attention as he walked toward him. "Where do you think the women are going to stay?"

He got no response.

"They don't know the area around here. They may not be safe."

Noah was surprised at the question. "I have no idea," he said, giving Jake a puzzled look.

"We should let them know what's around here, don't you think?" Jake lifted a quizzical eyebrow.

Noah tried to hide his discomfiture. "Of course." He gave a couple of hits with the hammer before saying, "I thought I'd check along the beach after we finish this project."

"Want company?" Jake asked.

"Nah. Best I talk to my *wife—see* what they intend."

What the heck is their intent? he asked himself. The question only added to his growing apprehension.

Noah finally put down the hammer as the day's work came to an end. He started down the beach in the direction the women had ridden. The tug he felt he tried to ignore. But he couldn't block out how drawn to Brit he felt, not just physically, but to her energy, her spirit.

* * *

Brit left the cove where they had set up their campsite and walked alone toward the ocean. She breathed in the tangy salt air and felt the rhythm of the waves' ebb and flow. So different from the desert.

Arms crossed across her chest in a kind of self-hug, she let herself just be. They were here—wherever here was. She didn't want to worry or even think where their next step would take them. It would be whatever it would be. *The Circle sure has its work cut out for it!* She couldn't repress a smile at the irreverent thought.

She was so lost in thought she didn't sense Noah's approach. When she turned to return to the others, she gasped in surprise when she saw him, concerned she hadn't felt Noah's presence. To hide her response, she turned away from him, toward the ocean.

He came up beside her, and without saying anything, he mirrored her and turned to face the ocean. After a few moments, he said, "Why, Brit?"

She looked down at her feet and then turned toward him. "The Shift," she said. She studied his reaction.

"The Shift?"

"We talked about it, don't you remember?"

"What are you talking about, Brit?"

"The Shift is real, Noah. The quakes have opened all of us, not just the earth. It's even happening to our animals."

He sat abruptly on the sand and tried to absorb what she was suggesting.

"I know how incredible this sounds," Brit said. "But you know me—without actual proof—"

"Stop! Just stop." He blurted, "I did not send you any message."

Brit sat down on the sand near him. She said nothing more—just looked out at the ocean.

"The others," he asked. "Do they all believe what you call The Shift?"

Softly, she said, "We are as One."

He got himself up off the sand, not sure whether to stay or leave. His heart was pounding. He wanted to run, get away—not from Brit, but from what she was saying.

Brit stood up, brushing off the sand. "You were right, Noah—about building the dome, making sure we were ready for any emergency."

She took another breath. Then facing him, she said, "You were right about The Gathering—or at least about most of the Elders." She looked into his eyes and said, "You protected us, Noah. I am so sorry it took the Big

One to literally shake me awake."

Noah started to walk away, then he turned back to say, "Jake and I will find a better place for all of you to stay." He took a deep breath, about to say more, but instead just stood, looking at her with what seemed a glimmer of hope on his face. His mouth opened, but then closed abruptly. He turned and started trotting back to his enclave.

Brit was calm, finally assured she had been right to come, whether Noah acknowledged it or not.

* * *

Jake had been busy while Noah was away. He retrieved the largest tent of those that had been left after the structure for the survivors was ready. No longer needed, he figured it would serve the women. He had scouted the area nearby and found a somewhat secluded spot for the tent. Now he just had to wait for Noah.

He whistled a tune as he watched for him. Having these women around would certainly spice up the place.

CHAPTER 23

When Brit got back to their camp, she found all the usual tasks had been completed. Lilla seemed back to her old self, complaining that this trip was all for nothing.

Gemma just rolled her eyes and let her vent. Risa was sacked out on her pallet, while Misha was lost in her own world.

Brit stood at the entrance of their improvised tent, smiling at her sisters. Then, sniffing, she got a whiff of something delicious. She moved to the fire pit and helped herself to the stew someone had made.

Gem saw the spring in her movements. "Noah found you?"

Brit, no longer surprised at how Gemma always Knew, brought her food over, and sat beside her. "Yes, he did," she said, as she savored the rich smell of the stew. "He is very confused." After a couple of bites, she continued, "He's not ready to acknowledge The Shift, even though it's working on him. I think it scares him," she said.

"So?"

"So, I can't know what's next for the two of us." She took Gem's hand for a moment, then returned to her meal. "I only know about our work." She gestured with her left arm, indicating the whole group. "Our work is my life now."

Gem nodded, but said, "And do you know what that is?"

Brit laughed, "No more than you do. But I believe we will be shown, or we will find it ourselves." She put down her empty bowl. "I only know that at this moment, I'm exhausted, and I am going to sleep until I wake up."

She wiped the bowl clean with sand and then went to her pallet to lie down. "It had better be a dire emergency before anyone wakes me," she said.

She was almost asleep when Gem said, "Sleep well, Brit. We all deserve it."

* * *

Noah jogged along the water's edge, hoping exercise would jar loose some understanding of what was happening. He realized he had been living in a kind of made-up world, focused only on that day's work. It had been his way to block out the guilty feelings he had about leaving Brit to fend for herself up North.

He recalled the intense longing in his dreams about her. She seemed so bereft, alone but still unable or unwilling to trust him, to see what he saw. He would wake up with clenched teeth and an ache in his gut, a foggy head, and only be able to alleviate his misery with the work.

He slowed his jog to a fast walk. *Brit looked and sounded so at peace. She was still so very lovely, even after traveling for days? Weeks?*

The Shift. He stopped, letting the small edges of the waves wash over his shoes. They had talked about The Shift in their early days in The Gathering when everything had seemed possible.

Slowly, he started walking again as he remembered their closeness and recollected their talks.

What was The Shift? They had laughed as they imagined how it would be to simply Know each other's thoughts. Would they Hear each other's words? How would that be? Could they refuse to be read? Would they have a block of some sort?

Then he remembered how they just stopped talking and began touching—

He started jogging again, the memory was too exquisitely painful. What had they lost? And why? And what now?

When he reached the enclave, he saw Jake pulling something huge out of the makeshift storage area. He sped up to join him with what he was attempting.

"Jake, hold on," he yelled. "I'll help." As he approached him, he asked, "What is this? What are we pulling?"

Jake laughed his welcome, "A tent. For the beautiful ladies you just went to visit."

"What?"

Between his grunts, as he attempted to move the folded up tent, Jake told Noah about the perfect space he'd found where they could set up the tent for the women. It was nearby.

Noah stopped pulling. "I'm not sure that is a good idea—"

"Sure it is," said Jake. "They'll be able to help with projects, and the work will go much faster." He pulled again before adding, "And it will be a lot more fun!" He saw Noah's expression. "Or interesting," he amended.

"Come on! They can't stay on the beach!" He started pulling and dragging again.

Noah shrugged and joined his efforts. "So where is this 'perfect' space?" he asked. Then added, "What makes you think that this is what they want?"

"Oh, just stop," said Jake, a twinkle in his eye. "Come on, Noah. You felt it. I know you have—or you —we wouldn't be here!"

Noah was caught off guard by Jake's comment. He dropped his part of the tent.

Jake clapped him on his back. "Don't worry about it. Let's just get this tent set up. They'll need it by tomorrow."

Without knowing why he was going along with Jake's instructions, Noah just did.

He made only one more objection, "Don't you think we should ask them first?"

"Not necessary," Jake said. "They'll Know."

* * *

Misha, still in her own world, saw that everyone was exhausted. They hadn't even considered making their Circle that evening. And it was all right.

She, on the other hand, needed to explore the next move toward their mission, to serve—how?

She was relaxed but energized as she fell deeper into her meditation. A tent? She let it evolve. *Who was this new person with Noah? Why do I feel I know him?* No one came into her mind. But she knew it was more than just a sense of new male energy.

She Knew they would move to a tent—tomorrow. It was important to their survival. More would evolve from this move.

She fell into a deeper unconscious state, a sleep she needed as much as did her sisters.

At dawn, a hum emerged from each of them. Somewhat surprised, they all looked to Misha for an explanation.

She said, "We need to pack, load the horses, and return to Noah's place on the beach. They have a place ready for us."

Without questioning, they quickly rose, packed, and left. As they mounted, they saw rough, choppy waves threatening to overrun their campsite.

It felt like a short ride to the enclave where they saw that workers were up and about. Coming toward them on horseback was Jake.

He shouted to the women as they dismounted, "Good morning! Breakfast is almost ready. You can stable your horses nearby." He dismounted and turned to them and said, "I'll show you. Then, after we eat, we'll show you to your new quarters."

They looked around for Noah, but he wasn't in sight.

Misha had been the first to dismount. She approached Jake, extending her hand to him. He took it in both of his.

She said to him, "Thank you. I'm Misha. We have met before."

"Yes," he said. "Indeed we have." He gave her a gentle smile.

"Come, Ladies. I'll lead you to the stables, and then, breakfast!"

"You wouldn't happen to have coffee, would you?" asked a hopeful Gemma.

"Sorry! But we do have a reasonable substitute." Jake laughed as he led them off.

Risa was grateful for the improvised stable as well as for the oats and hay provided for their horses. But she was puzzled. Didn't Jake recognize her? She felt uneasy to find him here, although he seemed very different—not the brash cowboy he tried to be when he first came to her ranch.

Feeling somewhat reassured, she happily joined the others as they departed for the structure where eggs and potatoes were being dished up. *Interesting, how now he seems to have eyes only for Misha.*

Brit was concerned that they would be taking rations provided for the workers here. Jake appreciated her concern but assured her that they were more than welcome to share.

Noah showed up as they were finishing. He seemed a little disheveled and somewhat neutral in his welcome. "We've finished setting up quarters for all of you. Thanks to Jake." He chose not to look at Brit.

Jake laughed again. Giving Noah a funny look, he said, "Yes, I am Jake! And I am delighted to welcome you here." The women smiled, appreciating his sense of humor, making them feel at ease.

Jake continued, "We figured you wouldn't be very

comfortable bunking here with everyone on the floor." He shared a look with Misha, which she acknowledged with a slight nod.

Then to her sisters' surprise, she responded, "It has come just in time. The waves were threatening to overrun our campsite."

"Well—let's show you to your safer abode." Jake's manner, in contrast to Noah's brooding look, was playful.

As they began following Jake's lead, Noah pulled Brit aside. "I hope you don't mind that we took the initiative."

"Of course not," she said. "Once again—you protected us." She put a hand on his arm and gave him a warm smile as she hurried to catch up with the others.

The new structure and the nearby tent were both on a rise which protected them from the tides. A tsunami could wipe everything out. But even the last one had left some of the structure intact. That had been enough to decide to build on the same site.

The tent was watertight and certainly would be much warmer than what they had been used to on their long journey.

As they looked around, they each expressed their appreciation, it was Brit who asked the question on each mind: "How may we serve?"

It was a simple question. But it struck Jake and even Noah as uniquely profound in its simplicity.

It was Jake who answered, "That will be revealed."

Noah looked at him. His questions now were about Jake.

CHAPTER 24

Noah seemed to be at a loss about what the women could do. Jake, once again, took over, suggesting that they tour the structure being built, meet, and talk with the people working here. See what called to them.

At first, the women were unsure how best to go about this. Risa was the first to stake out her area of expertise —the animals. From there, it was obvious the work would be different for each of them.

They were hesitant at first at being on their own. They soon realized that their shared mission—to serve —never changed. They agreed with Misha that they should meet every evening in their Circle. It seemed a simple decision.

Lilla found a group who got together to sing and often entertained 'the troops' as they put it. She wasn't sure that her choice qualified as serving. Her sisters happily told her to go for it!

Brit had a fast introduction to the medical team. Unexpectedly, a boy was brought in by his mother, coughing and wheezing from the constant dust stirred up by the quakes. His extreme discomfort called to Brit.

Intuitively, she reached out to the mother. "May I help?" she asked.

The boy's mother felt Brit's deep concern and nodded her permission. Brit went to the boy. She felt a warm vibration filling her hands, and she gently lay her hands on his chest. She drew on her Knowing and began to release her energy into the boy. His spasms ceased, and slowly, he started breathing normally. Brit's heart filled with gratitude.

As she monitored the boy's recovery, she questioned herself, *is this my 'new' power? How amazing; how wonderful*, she thought, as tears filled her eyes.

The boy's mother cried her relief and thanks. The medics asked Brit to please join in their efforts to care for people. Their meager equipment and supplies made medical care very limited. Her gift was a godsend.

Brit was so happy to embrace this mission.

By the second day, Gemma still had not found where she belonged. She made the rounds throughout the compound. In several places, she observed workers scurrying to find tools or supplies they needed, but weren't readily at hand.

Such wasted effort, she thought and wondered who was in charge. Was anyone in charge?

She talked with one or two men who seemed to be guiding different projects. Each indicated that they just saw what needed to be done and found other volunteers to help.

That did seem to be working. She asked herself whether more organization would help? She decided to get Jake's input.

When she found him, he was deep in conversation with Misha.

Interesting! She wasn't sure whether or not to interrupt. As she was about to leave, she heard Misha call, "Gemma! Join us, please."

Jake stood, "Please, Gemma. We would like your feedback."

Misha said, "I was just telling Jake what each of us is doing. Have you found your spot yet?"

Her eager enthusiasm warmed Gem's heart.

"Maybe. Actually—I was looking for Jake. I have an

idea."

"Please tell!" said Jake.

Gem described what she had surmised after studying how the workforce operated. "I'm wondering whether more organization would be more functional, more efficient." She assured Jake, "How well the present system works is laudable—*if it could be called a system*—"

"But?"

Gem shared some of her observations.

Jake listened carefully, offering no clear response until she was finished. "What do you suggest?" he asked.

"Perhaps we could bring the workers together, ask them for their ideas, what projects are now in play, what other projects need to be started. Find out who wants to work on which projects and find out who has skills—and whether they could teach others—"

Jake held up his hand and then smiled. "I see what you are getting at. Wonderful ideas, but maybe not all at once."

Gemma nodded, waiting for Jake's insight.

"Noah would be good at getting everyone together. Everyone knows and respects him. What do you think?"

Gemma hadn't considered Noah's position here or understood where he fit. She looked to Misha for her opinion.

Misha took Gem's hand. "I think your working with Noah is perfect. He will come to understand us."

Gem gave a one-shoulder shrug. "I hope so." She knew that she was not Noah's favorite person. Revealing her skepticism, she said, "Sure. I can take notes or something."

Admiring this redhead's spunk, Jake laughed before saying, "I think your partnership will be very productive."

That evening the group had their Circle for the first time in the tent. Afterword, they shared experiences; what it was like working with the new groups. Brit was surprised but enthusiastic about Gem working with Noah.

"Are you sure?" Gem asked. "We don't have the most positive history together."

"We were very different people," Brit said.

"I know the five of us have become—whatever we are. Do you think Noah—?"

"Gem, his arrogance is gone. He's opening, whether

he knows it or not. Working with you will feel safe for him. He can grow to trust who we have become."

The others murmured their approval. Gem acquiesced.

Misha acknowledged she didn't have an assigned work role.

"You seemed to be connecting to Jake," Gem said with a knowing smile.

"Yes," she answered.

Brit spoke up, "Misha, what did you mean when you said to Jake, 'We've met before'?"

Lilla cut in, "Yeah, and he said 'Indeed we have.' What was that about?"

Misha stayed very still, saying nothing. The sisters waited.

"I know him from the old Gathering."

Brit said, "I don't remember him. Where did—?"

Misha shook her head. "No, he didn't belong. Although I didn't either, sort of."

Brit was puzzled. "Sort of?"

"I never fully embraced all that the Elders were preaching. They thought I did because I never said anything. At that time, I had no other place to go," she explained, "So, I stayed… until the upheavals got to be too much."

Misha sighed and then finally gave in to their inquiries.

"I used to do a walking meditation in the park. One day, he began walking next to me—and we Heard each other." She looked at their rapt faces. "It was wonderful to be with someone who understood."

"Understood what?" asked Risa.

"The Shift—it meant connection. I didn't know that before." She stopped. A full minute passed.

In that minute, Risa knew she didn't want to acknowledge that she also had met Jake.

Misha went on, "Then he disappeared—until we met here. I know the Circle of Intent brought us together—then and now."

Brit was the one to ask, "What do you think that means, Misha?"

"I don't know… yet. We have just begun to talk." Another sigh escaped her lips. She changed the subject back to their missions, "I want to work with the other women, but they seem to resent my intrusion." Misha hung her head.

Gem said, "Well, that's their problem!"

Misha smiled at her. "But how can we reach others if

that negativity gets in the way?"

Brit stood. "That is what each of us must work out. What we need right now is rest."

The Circle of Sisters disbanded for the night. Tomorrow would be a new beginning for each of them.

CHAPTER 25

Noah set out at dawn. He was going inland for the first time in many months. He left a message for Jake that he wanted to evaluate progress for the hoped-for cleanup of the main streets.

His real motivation was to get away from the women, especially Brit. But he also wanted to figure out what was Jake's relationship to the women.

It felt good to be walking away from the compound. Noah investigated partially collapsed buildings, determining what might be salvageable. Little of value seemed to remain.

He met a few people who had put together small compounds, similar to their own enclave. He also asked for news. What was happening in the rest of the paralyzed city, the state, or the country? It was at the food centers that he got some information.

The government 'copters that brought in supplies for the survivors brought news that more and more people were being ferried out of the quake zones to communities far inland. There were conditions, however. The refuges had to agree to support with their labor whichever community accepted them.

To Noah, this suggested that the center of the quake was very close to Los Angeles. He also heard that the tsunami had wiped out the southern beach communities closest to the Mexican border.

Strange, he thought. Why was their small enclave saved, while others were wiped out? It felt selective, although he dismissed that idea as nonsense.

He learned from other supply centers that much of the country had been hit with disasters: wildfires raged in the West; volcanoes were erupting all around the so-called ring of fire; Italy's long-dormant volcanoes were once again active; hurricanes of unparalleled force were pounding the East Coast.

The Federal government was stretched beyond its capacity to do anything except provide food and limited mobile housing. Survival was the only priority.

The one positive news came from the Imperial Valley, the breadbasket of the country. Not completely devastated by the quakes, their food production had stayed intact. Which was why food was being distributed by helicopters to sites made available to those still left in the doomed city.

By the end of the day, Noah concluded that their home in the North was ultimately the place to re-establish a viable community. The dome had validated his ideas. But, *what about Brit? I don't even know how I feel, let alone figure out what she wants.*

On his way back to the enclave, he realized he had to come to some resolution with Brit. Noah knew that neither of them were the same people. He also admitted to himself that the qualities that drove him crazy, her stubborn determination and refusal to acknowledge the power of negativity, that she could see only the good in people—even in the Elders!—these were the exact characteristics that were needed to build a new community.

Where did he fit into this scheme of things?

He knew that the dreaded conversation with Brit had to happen soon. He picked up his pace, grateful that he hadn't discovered any bodies in his exploration.

CHAPTER 26

Jake invited Misha to join him in a meditation.

"Happily," she said with a big smile.

He started to tell her his concerns: "Noah and Brit are needed as a couple to rebuild—or rather build a new kind of community. This enclave is a beginning, perhaps could even be a model…" He stopped when she reached out her hand to get his attention.

"I Know," she said. She waited for him to tune-in to her vibration.

Jake chuckled. Of course. He felt he was already in tune with this sensitive.

Misha realized she had to overcome her resistance to fully sharing with Jake. Her commitment to the Circle of Intent came even before him or any hope of their being together.

She expanded her energy, and for the first time, she

allowed his energy fully to merge with hers. Their energetic connection nearly overwhelmed her. She so much wanted to share the Circle of Intent with Jake. Holding her breath, she held a space for him to absorb the possible enormous implications of The Shift.

He was stunned at first. He had to sit with this. What would it mean to build a community with this kind of transparency? He knew The Shift had happened. *Was it happening with everyone? Total transparency? Was that possible, or even good? What was this Circle—of women? Why were they here, and to what end?*

This was so much more than he had allowed himself to imagine. Who were these women?

Misha waited for Jake to re-emerge from their connection. He took a deep breath and then let it go slowly and evenly. He opened his eyes, releasing Misha's energy as he did.

She took his hands in hers. "Now, you understand?"

"Not hardly," he said. "I still don't know who—all of you are, or why you came here."

His reaction took her aback. Breathlessly, she said, "I believe we are here to rebuild. This is a new beginning." She stuttered her next words, "I don't think we stay here, though. We will move on, but when or where has not been revealed."

"Revealed? By whom?"

"No, no. Not like that." She wasn't sure how to explain the Circle of Intent. *Why hadn't he Heard?* "No one leads or directs us. It is us; only more than us." She trembled with frustration that he did not See or Know this.

Jake took her in his arms to reassure her quietly. Speaking into her ear, he said, "Let me sit with this for awhile." Still holding her arms, he gently pulled back from her. "It's a lot to take in." He smiled as he stroked her cheek with his thumb and then left.

He had to find Noah. Talk to him about these women. After all, Noah knew them. Maybe he could explain what they were about.

Why didn't he understand? Misha knew their energies had merged. So, why?

She retreated back to their tent, where she found Gemma, sitting cross-legged, hunched over her organizational models.

Gem looked up as Misha entered and immediately rose and pulled her into a warm embrace before she sat her down. "I just made some tea. The water's still hot; I'll make you a cup of your favorite ginger tea."

She handed Misha her tea and sat down beside her. "Now tell me. What are you so upset about?"

Misha tried to compose herself, although tears filled her eyes as she told Gem about her meeting with Jake. "How could he not understand the Circle of Intent? He just called us a circle—of women! He pulled his energy away from me as if he were afraid… of me. Of us."

Gem listened. This was instructive. Not everyone was experiencing The Shift in the same way. What might that mean?

Gem continued to consider the implications as she held Misha's hands while she told her story. When Misha finished, Gem held her as she wept.

Gemma realized that Misha thought of Jake as her soul mate. Her hopes seemed dashed, but maybe not. Time would reveal more.

* * *

Their Circle that evening was focused and intense. Each had experienced peoples' suspicion and even hostility in some quarters.

"I know," Brit acknowledged. "It happened to me, too. All of a sudden, people were suspicious, asking where did my gifts come from?"

Gemma asked, "Do you think they were afraid of losing status, or maybe just not feeling valuable anymore?"

"I don't know, but it took a lot of effort to block out their energy lashing at me. I'm exhausted. And listening to Misha's experience is not reassuring."

Gem nodded in sympathy. "I decided it was better to work on my models here in the tent." She, too, had run into opposition. "My attempts to engage others in dialog about functionality and efficiency were not welcomed."

The Shift seemed to be sporadic, and this surprised them.

Their harmonic hum that night became full-voiced, embracing, healing, and it energized each of them.

The ethereal sound reached Noah's ears as he entered the compound. He followed it to the entrance of their tent. He stood listening and watching, captivated by the blue-green energy field that swirled around the women as they sang without words. As it faded away, the women together rose and stood upright in a mutual trance.

Noah's incredulous voice broke their concentrated focus.

"What are you? A bunch of witches?"

As he ran off, Brit called out, "Noah!"

In his haste, he didn't see Jake until he almost ran into him.

"Hey, Man! Where are you off to so fast?" Jake snagged him as they almost collided.

"Not now, Jake," Noah said, almost careening into a bench.

"Yeah, now! What's happened?"

Noah shook his head and tried to release his arm from Jake's strong grip.

"Stop. Just stop," Jake said as he clasped Noah into a firm hug.

Noah sank onto the nearby bench, and he finally released the crippling tension throughout his body.

"I don't know what is happening," he blurted. "The women—"

"Ah!" said Jake. "You heard their song."

"More than that—I saw—"

"Saw what?"

"You'll think I'm crazy—"

"I don't think so. Tell me."

"The energy—waves, binding them together, rising and falling with their voices—that unearthly sound—that could break your heart." He hung his head in his hands. "I called them witches."

Jake nodded, then smiled as he said, "I can see that." Then seeing Noah's expression, he said, "My reaction was pretty strong, too."

"You saw it too?"

"Not exactly. Misha—" He didn't know how to explain the energy connection that allowed them to merge, to Know—until he had backed away.

Looking directly at Noah, he explained. "The Shift is real, and it's happening in all of us and in everything—whether we believe in it or not—it is here. And Yes! It scares us."

Noah almost barked a laugh in agreement.

"But no, they are not witches or any other negative thing. But they are special, unique in our world. And apparently, they have a mission—one that includes us."

"How so?"

"I'm not sure, but you and Brit need to resolve the friction between you."

"I don't know, Jake, if—"

"I do," Jake cut off Noah's objection. "And I must repair my clumsy break away from Misha."

"Misha and you?"

"You don't walk away from your soul mate, Noah. Not if you have your wits about you."

Jake calmed himself. He needed to reassure Noah. "Just open your heart—your energy—to Brit. She will meet you."

"But—"

"Trust me."

After their Ceremony, Misha wanted to share her new realization with her sisters, and she was the first to speak. "Of course. We should have realized. Now we take for granted who we are within our Circle of Intent. But it's foreign to most people, it scares them. Even Jake was scared, and he has been working with The Shift in his own way for awhile."

"Maybe we should leave," said Lilla. "Scared people can be dangerous."

Gem retorted, "Running? We don't do that."

Risa asked, "Do you think we really are in danger?" She looked at each one. "Even some horse handlers have been standoffish with me, especially after Sunshine and I take each horse for a run along the beach. I thought they would be happy with what Sunshine can teach them." She slumped, discouraged.

Excited, Misha said, "I think—no, I Know—that we are fine. But maybe we forgot the Circle and depended on our own expertise too much. Let's refocus our energy to turn fear into positive acceptance from each person we meet. A few may want to join us."

"Empower others," said Brit. "Yes, I see what you are after."

Brit smiled as her heart opened again. She hadn't realized how hard and fast she had shut down at Noah's accusation. It was imperative to unite their energies. This was their mission—to empower each and all the people they meet.

They grasped one another's hands once more, letting their energies flow with each other.

Gem dismissed them with: "We begin tomorrow."

CHAPTER 27

Jake was persuasive. Noah had come to realize that he had overreacted. The Shift? It was hard to accept what had seemed unattainable, just something that might happen in the far distant future. And, there it was! In front of his eyes, while he was standing up, not dreaming.

Never would he have imagined that Brit would be part of—whatever the Circle was about. It was also impossible to believe she could be part of anything evil. She was stubbornly good.

Noah pushed his hands through his hair. How was he going to talk to Brit? And what about those other women? Did she know about Lilla?

His thoughts traveled around and around in his brain. How was he supposed to approach Brit? He tried to throw off these impossible issues by going for a run along the beach. The moon had risen, lighting his path. It felt good to be running.

A figure in the distance, near the water's edge, caught his attention. He slowed his pace to a walk as he came closer. "Brit," he called to her.

She turned to acknowledge him, her expression neutral, as was her body language. In the moonlight, she looked ethereal, unworldly. He found himself speechless as he gazed at her.

"Noah," she said. Waiting.

He stumbled through his first words of apology, accepting how off base he had been when first seeing and hearing the women in their Circle. But he needed to know what that—was.

"Of course you do," Brit said before he uttered the question. She seemed amused at his shocked expression.

"Let's walk," she said as she started moving along the water's edge, letting her feet touch the foam of the incoming waves.

Noah stepped up beside her. Still deep in thought, he muttered, "The Shift."

Brit nodded, "Yes, that's part of it." She continued walking. "But it seems you have to be open to it. I didn't know that before your—" She hesitated, but then spoke the word, "attack."

"I'm so sorry, Brit."

"I know," she interrupted, then stopped and looked at him, "Why is it that when women come together in a significant way, it's felt threatening—we must be witches or have some evil intent?"

He hardly knew how to respond. Was that true, he wondered? Is that why their 'ceremony' scared him? "Can you help me understand?" He hoped she would hear his sincere desire to know.

"Can you get past your judgments?" Brit asked.

Noah tensed before silently accepting her words. He nodded. Waiting.

"We are the Circle of Intent," she said. "We Survive to Serve."

He could see that she was monitoring his response, and he did his best to be neutral—whether he understood her or not.

Brit sat down on the sand, inviting him to do the same. She began telling him the story of their journey, what they discovered about themselves, who they had become together.

When she stopped, he asked, "And what about us, you and me? How do we fit—or do we fit—into this scenario?"

Brit took her time to answer. "I don't know." She glanced at him. "I like who I have become, myself, me —with my sisters." She sighed. "I think it must be determined by you—by your acceptance—or not. Whether you can—or will—open to our mission."

"Your mission?"

He could see her difficulty in trying to explain. He kept quiet and waited.

"Our mission—it's simply to serve. But it seems to change as needs arise. But we—my sisters—we always 'do'—almost before Knowing. And we 'do' as one."

"It sounds so—theoretical or—I don't know what to call it," Noah said.

"Yes, doesn't it!" she agreed. "I just mark it up to The Shift." She shrugged her shoulders in acceptance of whatever it was. She rose as if she were about to leave.

He reached out and clasped her hand. The sweetness coming from her was irresistible, and he drew her close to his chest. She came willingly. Then, gently she put her right hand next to his forehead and her left on his heart. She then pulled back to look into his eyes, and reversed her hands, placing her left beside his forehead, the right on his heart.

Puzzled at first, he then felt the vibration from her touch throughout his body, and he acquiesced to his sudden Knowing that flooded body and mind.

"Brit—"

"Shh. Just let me in," she whispered.

She softly touched his lids, and he closed his eyes, allowing the feelings and information to move through him.

"The Circle of Intent?" he questioned.

Brit nodded. "That's what we call it. Do you understand now?" she asked.

"I need to process—all this," he said.

Brit began to pull away.

"No—please. Don't go," he pleaded.

She stopped and then let him pull her close once more.

"I'm not rejecting, just trying to grasp—all of it."

Brit relaxed once again into his arms and said, "I know. It's OK." She then took a step back to look into his eyes. "All of us have had to absorb this Shift. And we have. Our journey facilitated the process for us.

"At times, it feels like magic—no wonder you called us witches." She chuckled although he flinched. "But it's not magic. It's unrevealed power within each of us —if we allow the revelation."

Brit extricated herself from his arms. "Go now, Noah. Please. We'll talk later—and you can talk with all of us." She smiled warmly at him, turned, and quickly walked back to the compound.

Noah watched her until she entered her tent. He let go of the breath he had been holding and began walking, watching the small waves lapping along the water's edge.

CHAPTER 28

Brit found Gem still working on her charts when she entered their tent.

"How did it go?" Gem's casual remark made Brit laugh.

"You know very well how it went," she said.

"Yes. But you can still talk about it if you like," Gem responded. "Sometimes, it helps."

Brit stood looking down at her. "I think we have to wait. His resistance surprises me."

"To The Shift or to you?"

"Good question. Maybe both." She sat down beside Gem, wrapping her arms around her legs, knees pulled to her chest, she said, "I do know our Circle, us together is what I want, what I need. Noah's and my relationship can never be what it was… Nor do I want it to be."

"Maybe you can create something new," she said.

Brit got up and made her way to her bed. "Better get some sleep, Gem."

* * *

"The Circle has to expand," Misha told them the following evening. They hadn't yet begun their ceremony. "We can't reach others unless we include others." Misha was adamant.

Lilla, with a cloudy face, interjected, "What if they don't want to be included? All they said to me today was that I'm too loud. I can't help it if I have a big voice," she exclaimed.

Her sisters smiled broadly. Risa took one hand, Misha the other, and said, "With our unity, they have no choice."

Misha continued, "As we sing, let's visualize a huge bubble that expands and wraps around the entire enclave. Let's fill it with our intent."

They began the hum.

* * *

The next morning to her surprise, Lilla found herself warmly welcomed into her choral group. More surprising to her was how effortlessly she found her voice blending with the others.

Risa was approached by two of the handlers as she entered the enclosure. They asked if they could accompany her with their horses when she rode. They wanted to know why, when their horses returned, they were so much easier to handle.

She Heard their sincerity. "I don't really 'do' anything," she said to them. "But, please do come."

Somehow Gem found the words and feelings she needed to persuade the admin group to be open to the changes she proposed.

Brit and Misha decided to try working together in the medical compound. Although they were determined to be very circumspect, they faced no objections. On the contrary, they were welcomed by the staff as they went from bed to bed, caring for, and healing patients.

That evening as they gathered to discuss that day's experiences, Brit asked, "Are we forcing them somehow? That doesn't feel right."

Risa insisted that the Circle wouldn't let them do

anything wrong. "It was so nice to have companions to ride with as Sunshine did whatever she does, instructing the other horses."

Lilla volunteered, "I didn't feel like I was fighting anyone today. And not one person complained about me. It felt good."

Gem nodded, "Me too. Others actually came up with some good ideas—and I Heard where they were coming from. Quite a different day."

Brit felt encouraged by everyone's input. Then added her own. "I loved working with Misha. I think we learned from each other, too," she said with a look at Misha, who nodded her agreement.

"Let's continue to expand," Misha said.

As their hum began, Brit wondered whether she should try to influence Noah. Then their song swallowed her up, and she gave in to the heightened vibration swirling through and among them as it expanded, enfolding the community they had joined.

CHAPTER 29

Jake found Misha working with Brit in the medical unit. Just watching her filled him with a kind of peaceful joy.

She raised her head and turned toward him. She smiled and then went back to her task. Brit finished and leaned toward Misha, whispering to her.

Misha nodded and removed her elastic gloves. She joined Jake, to his relief and pleasure.

"Yes, we should talk," she said silently.

Jake hid his surprise, reminding himself that this could be the new normal—unspoken, but Heard communication.

They exited the medical unit and strolled through the compound, exiting the door that led to the newly provided tables, a few chairs, and a bench on an improvised patio. The midmorning sun was warm, and they sat together on the bench, soaking it in.

"Jake, there is no need to apologize," Misha said, once more startling him.

"This seems to be more and more awkward," he said. That he was flummoxed by The Shift was ironic. But the power in Misha and these women had totally upset his preconceived ideas about a new society evolving out of the disaster of the mega-quakes.

He also felt how open he was to her, and this time it did not feel invasive. He hoped she would open to him.

She waited as he took three deep breaths and then slowly exhaled the last one. He let his energy find its way to her, gently probing until images flooded his imagination: five horsewomen, then a Circle; a joyous song-without-words, finally a stillness which evolved into 'We Survive to Serve. We are guided by our Circle of Intent.'

He breathed deeply once more. "I Heard and Saw you—all of you. Thank you."

"Good. Oh, Good," she said. "Now, you can join us."

"How do you mean?" he said a bit anxiously.

"I know your heart, and now your mind. You are a good man—and you can Hear us!"

Her eagerness made him pull back a little. Gently, he put his fingers on her lips. "How can I join with you…"

He paused, "… without knowing or understanding this 'intent?'"

She took a step back. "But you Know—you Heard!"

Jake wanted to reassure her. But he couldn't, not without fully grasping what the Intent was—or how the Circle guided. Was someone or something guiding this Circle? And to what end?

Good Lord, I sound like Noah! "Give me some time to absorb, process, experience all this," he finally said to her.

She took in a long breath. "OK," she said. "Just tell me when you've figured it out." She got up from the bench and returned to the medical unit.

Brit saw her as she came in. *Oh, dear. How are we ever going to get these two together?* She reached out to Misha and enfolded her in a big hug.

CHAPTER 30

That night Misha tossed and turned, restless. She finally got out of bed, and throwing on her cloak, she quietly left the tent. The stars were so bright they lit her way down to the water. She loved listening to the gentle waves breaking on the shore and then sweeping back into the ocean.

The salty tang filled her nostrils as she breathed deeply and then exhaled, trying to let go of her disappointment. This was the first time she doubted her convictions about The Shift.

When she first saw Jake, she felt she Knew him. She was sure he had experienced The Shift. Why wasn't he open to her?

She sat on the sand, head bowed, and resting on her knees. Time went by, but she felt timeless. Round and round, the questions rose. *What don't I Know or at least understand?*

She felt a quiver of anticipation. *What was—?*

Then she saw Jake as he sat down beside her and wrapped his arms around her.

She didn't know whether to rebuff or embrace him. So she just sat very still.

"You want closeness, touch, honesty," he spoke softly.

She was startled into recognizing that was exactly what she yearned for. But why did it leave her more confused than ever?

"Be patient. We all will get there in our own time."

"Jake—"

"Hush. Just let me in."

Suddenly, she realized he hadn't said a word aloud. She Heard and Felt him within her. Joy overtook her as she turned to see him more clearly. *Was this connection real?*

Jake nodded, smiling at her recognition and acceptance.

She let herself cry and move even closer into Jake's embrace. He held her close, identifying with her confusion and longing—and remembering.

How different from everyone Jake felt growing up, trying to hide his growing perceptions about friends and even family. The latter was more painful. To say they didn't 'get him' was mild compared to the outright rejection he felt.

His parents were very conservative, hard-working, blue-collar people. They couldn't hide their incomprehension at who he was or their fear for him. His sensitivity dismayed them because they didn't understand it. Why didn't he play football or at least baseball? Why didn't he make friends? They were sure the kids at school would want to hang out with him. He preferred being alone. Why?

He learned how to appear happy-go-lucky, to be fast with laughing at stupid jokes, buddy-buddying. None of it was real. It just helped him get through his young years.

He could feel Misha Hearing and understanding.

The memory of the Big One surfaced. He had Known something 'big' was brewing. But nothing, not even the mini-quakes had prepared him for when it hit him— literally.

He was thrown from the building he was about to enter. A geyser erupted a short distance away, and everything nearby was blown upward and out.

He was unconscious when he was found by helpers looking for survivors. Amazingly, although he was badly bruised, nothing was broken.

As he was healing, he began Knowing in a way quite different from before the Mega-quake. He Knew he had to heal in order to help. Eventually, that led him to the food center where he met up with Noah.

Misha hugged Jake tightly, her tears finally exhausted. He had come away from his memories to her once again.

The tide brought the waves closer and closer to them. It was time to move, which they did together.

"What now, Little Mouse?" Jake asked.

"Little Mouse? I'm not so little," she said.

"My fierce, yet sensitive, adorable little mouse, who means so much to me," he said as he gazed tenderly into her upturned face.

"Hm," she responded, starting to walk once again.

They slowly made their way toward the compound, enjoying the sun that was finally breaking through the morning fog.

Misha still wasn't sure she liked that nickname, but from Jake, it sounded sweet—and comforting.

* * *

Risa opened her eyes, feeling wide awake. She had to make sense of her dream. Was it real? She rose and quickly dressed.

Good! She saw that Brit had already left the tent, and that Gem was awake, doing her morning stretches to get the kinks out. Misha was gone.

"Gem," she called to her silently.

Gem looked up and spotted Risa. She beckoned her over.

"What's up?" she asked, finishing her last stretch.

"I think Carlos is calling me—in my dream time."

Gem stopped and gave Risa her full attention. "What was the message?"

"How do I know if it was a message? Maybe it was just a dream."

"Just tell me what he said," urged Gemma.

"He appeared first, beckoning me home. Then he said I'm needed there. 'People are waiting.'"

"I see." Gem sat with it for a few minutes. "Let's discuss this with everyone at the Circle this evening."

"Should I—"

"Wait until this evening. Take Sunshine for a ride.

Pick up her vibe—"

At Risa's perplexed expression, she said, "Just stay open."

Risa nodded acceptance.

"It's going to be fine," Gem said. "It always is. Right?"

"OK." Risa reached out and gave Gem a hug. "I've got to get to work," she said as she straightened up. "Thanks."

Gemma finished dressing as she mulled over this latest development. She was not certain that Risa wasn't just homesick for her horses, her ranch—and maybe for Carlos.

The Circle should be interesting tonight. I wonder what Misha will make of this.

Gem was gratified that the few changes the admin group had implemented were speeding up progress on the structure and improving morale.

Maybe their mission here was done. That Risa was receiving messages was unusual, but felt authentic.

Brit and Noah were still an uncertainty. Lilla was happy for now. Her group was preparing for a concert of sorts, and she was very involved. What about Misha?

And Jake? She didn't know, although she Felt a resolution had been reached.

Her own sense told her that she had work elsewhere waiting, but no clarity as to what that would be. *Well, the morning awaits!* She made her way to the camp kitchen for coffee—*and maybe today an egg.*

* * *

That evening the Circle began as usual, but paused before their song began when Misha held up her hand, "We need to share—and then define our Intent."

Gem encouraged Risa to begin. She told them about her dream of Carlos—and then what her ride with Sunshine revealed. "It's time to go—all of us. That's what I Heard."

No one spoke until Gemma looked to Lilla, who at first gave an 'I don't know' shrug, but finally said, "I need to experience this musical event we're preparing." She hesitated but then went on: "The boys—I'm missing them. I don't think they miss me, but—there is more to be done at home."

All Misha said was that she and Jake had connected, but she wasn't sure yet what that might mean.

They all waited for Brit, who finally said, "I love Noah, but I can't wait for him if we must leave. This—us—we are what matters most to me." She stopped and wrapped her arms around herself tightly.

She trembled slightly before speaking again. "Each of you has a history with Noah. I know that—and so do you," she said firmly. "I'm assured that whatever that connection—or desired connection was—has been changed as we have changed. Am I right, or am I once again deluding myself?"

She looked at each one to gain access clearly to each one's intention. No one avoided her eyes.

Lilla blushed when Brit looked directly at her. "It didn't mean anything—just that I could. I know that was stupid, but it's true." She took a deep breath before going on. "I resented that he loved you. I didn't think you really loved him. Or at least that's how I justified the fling or whatever it was. I didn't know then that it could hurt you. I could never do that now."

"Thank you," Brit said, before turning her attention to the others. "Yes, I hear each of you. We truly are One."

Gem then said, "Clearly, there is still unfinished business here. I sense, however, that we shall be leaving soon. Perhaps we should begin preparations."

Misha said, "Let the Circle begin," and began the hum once again.

As their meditation deepened, each Heard the same message:

Expand and solidify this Circle. Empower and praise the new practitioners. Let each one discover the power within. No need to designate power as The Shift. It is what it is.

This time, when their Circle was done, the women remained sitting, absorbing the message through the filter of their personal talents, skills, and desires as well as their sense of mission. Their intent had become personal as well as their one unified intention to serve. This blending of their group's mission with their own goals felt different. It felt right. They had survived by caring and supporting one another, putting service at the center of their lives, as well as serving individually the larger community.

Now, each experienced the urgency to complete their missions here.

Risa broke their silence. "Let's get going!"

* * *

Lilla's choral concert was wonderful fun and, at times, very meaningful. Her own participation spurred everyone else's enthusiasm. Throughout the rehearsal time, she gathered as many of their songs as she could remember and then sing. She had visions of her boys and many others doing musical performances.

A few singers asked about her sisters, and what it was they were singing every night. What made them so special? Some asked to meet them, and those who came asked if they could join.

Risa often took two and sometimes three of the stabled horses out for runs along the beach. She needed no reins or leads. Watching Diablo and Cloud run together was awe-inspiring. Sunshine seemed to convey to Blaze and Ginger the moves needed to support the stallion and mare as they created their intricate patterns.

Workers gathered at the doors and windows to watch with Risa how Sunshine put them through their paces. They burst into applause as they watch them finish by running full tilt down the waterfront.

Risa's sense of urgency infected her sisters' efforts and inspired the volunteers working on the structure. As the work was coming to an end, Gemma and her new colleagues started making plans for nearby broken down buildings that could be turned into temporary shelters.

Gem focused on training emerging leaders, providing them with organizational tools and practical tips for organizing and motivating a group to work harmoniously together. Mainly, she wanted them to believe in themselves and trust each other.

People were more and more drawn to the beautiful songs without words that came from the women's tent each evening.

Brit and Misha made a point of opening up the flaps of the tent after each Circle, inviting those who came to listen to come in and partake of the buffet they had prepared. The women were happy to informally answer questions as they arose. And anyone who asked to join their 'singing' was warmly welcomed.

CHAPTER 31

Noah kept himself busy. The structure was progressing well. He was impressed with the changes implemented by the admin group. This project was going to be finished soon.

Then what? For him?

Many of the volunteers gathered to hear the women 'singing,' but he stayed on the fringes. He was always a loner, but he nevertheless craved companionship. That had been the initial attraction of The Gathering. And as the Elders entrusted him more and more, he had thrived.

The principle of service made sense to him: you get back what you put in. That is until it was corrupted by certain leaders who sought disciples to do their bidding. Had he done that? He hoped not.

What about those women with Brit? *Or was she with*

them?

Lilla—pure lust, especially before Brit, would look in his direction. And Risa? Always inviting him to the ranch—and he went… only because he was curious.

The memory triggered a thought: what a great place for a small community to grow from. *Whew! Where did that come from?* He shook off that kind of thinking.

And Misha—Jake called her 'Little Mouse,' but Noah could feel her power. He hadn't seen that before. He had felt the need to protect her somehow. *Yeah— from those Elders. Good thing they were gone. All those fancy words—the coming of The Shift that would keep everyone honest—sure and easily manipulated by the Elders!*

He had felt their intrusive methods himself. *Well, if The Shift was all about manipulation, he wanted no part! Was that why their Circle repulsed him? Fear they could—would manipulate? But why would Brit—?*

He grabbed his shirt and stalked off the worksite. He needed answers.

Jake ran into Noah just as he exited the compound.

"Hey—Noah—where are you off to?"

Noah just waved and kept on walking. Jake hesitated,

then went after him. He came up beside him. Neither spoke until Noah slowed and then stopped.

"Are you now one of them?" Noah snarled.

Jake looked directly at Noah. "Them? Who is them?"

Noah huffed, then took in a breath, about to yell at Jake—until he stopped himself.

"I—I don't know what to think—or what to believe."

"Yeah, I get that."

They both moved to sit on a small grassy knoll that overlooked the ocean.

Jake spoke, "They were all part of The Gathering, right?"

Noah stole a look at Jake, "Yeah."

Jake opened further, to better sense Noah's confusion. "They seem different now though, huh?"

"Maybe."

"Hard to let go of old ideas," Jake said, a neutral energy coming from him.

Noah practically spat out, "All I saw from certain Elders was the attempt to manipulate the women especially—and they pulled me in with their promises…"

"*They* pulled you in?" Jake asked.

Noah's scrambled thoughts started to come together as he contemplated what Jake was saying. "OK, nobody *made* me do anything. It wasn't as if they gave permission. It was more like a taste of power—and it was exhilarating—until it wasn't."

He put his head down, feeling sheepish. "When I bedded Lilla, I knew how dishonest it was. I hated myself—and the Elders."

"Easier to hate them, I suppose," said Jake.

"Yeah, I guess. But do you see how destructive this business with The Shift is?"

"Can be. Up to us." Jake got up, gave Noah a pat on the back, and started back to the compound.

Noah sat, wrestling with his demons. Somehow, Jake had given him ammunition with which to fight them.

* * *

Brit was rearranging her hair that got tangled in the cap she wore for protection while working in the Med. Center, when Noah suddenly came up to her.

He blurted, "What if I just want to take you to bed?"

Shocking herself, she retorted, "That's not a terrible idea," but then looked at his exasperated expression. What was happening? She gave him a tentative smile and placed her hand gently on his arm.

He shook it off. "What if I just want to use you?" he barked.

"You can't do that," she said calmly. "I would Know your motive."

That answer stopped him. He considered what she was saying.

"So, that's your protection," he slowly articulated, to himself more than to her.

"Exactly," she said.

He abruptly left. Brit stood and watched him leave. She smiled.

CHAPTER 32

Noah considered a swim in the ocean to wick off his tension. Not alone. Not at night. The volunteers had made those rules for themselves. Too much debris to be safe—still.

Maybe Jake would come with him. No, he would just want to talk. *Was that fair to Jake?* Forget it; Noah didn't want to think about anything.

As he jogged, he caught sight of Jake with Misha. He slowed to a walk and just looked at Jake, holding her—so tenderly. He quickly moved along. *Was that possible for him and Brit?* He wanted it to be, he admitted to himself.

He had wanted the dome he had built to make her feel safe, even though she had scoffed at the idea before he went ahead and had it built. He wanted her respect. And he wanted her to admit he was right! That thought stopped him in his tracks. Why did that matter?

More than anything, he wanted her passion to be for him, not some utopia. She had rejected The Gathering or at least the Elders. But then she became so sad, even despondent, and she had closed herself off from him. He had to leave. To stay had become too painful.

He'd found a place here for his skills. He was reasonably content—and then she came here, disrupting his life… Again!

He jogged faster, then slowed again as he thought about how different she seemed now. Could that difference include hope for the two of them? He sank down on the sand, catching his breath as he struggled with his memories.

"Noah?"

Startled, he looked up. "Brit?"

"Can I help?"

"I don't need a lecture!" he exploded.

"Of course not," she said, her face showing the hurt.

"I'm sorry." He stood up, hardly able to disguise his chaotic emotions. "This may not be the best time to talk."

"Maybe it's the *best* time—we can be honest."

He felt her probing, almost like a gentle knocking within. Did he want to let her in?

She withdrew her energy and waited for his acceptance.

"Brit, why can't you accept my love?" his voice almost strangled with unexpressed feelings of hurt and confusion.

"Who says I can't?" She moved into his arms and planted a kiss on his unresponsive lips.

Before she could pull away, he pulled her in and gave her a kiss of his own.

"Come on," he said, and he took her hand and began jogging. "I know a place."

He took her cloak she had wrapped around herself, and he spread it out on the dry sand in the small cove hidden behind a tall rock outcropping. He beckoned her to sit beside him. She knelt down and then let him pull her into his embrace.

He held her against his heart, stroking her—but momentarily stopped to ask, "You do want me, yes?"

"Oh, yes," she breathlessly answered as she began frantically to remove her clothes.

He held her arms. "Slowly," he said. "Let me."

He murmured as the final bit of clothing came off. "Oh, Brit…"

"Shh—please—I want you so much," she echoed.

He couldn't hold back his desire for her any longer and entered her body—and her mind with an urgency he couldn't control and found her passion fully meeting his.

Exhausted, but thrilled with this new discovery of each other, they lay in each other's arms.

When the tide threatened to bring the waves too close, they untangled from each other, laughing as they quickly pulled on garments flung aside.

He pulled her up into his arms for a warm kiss before snatching her cloak from the sand. He shook off the sand before pulling her cloak around her, ending with another kiss.

Looking at her glowing face, he hardly dared to believe what he Knew.

"Just accept the Truth of it," she said, but not aloud.

It was so strange to actually communicate this way. Her love was so much more than their coupling. How could he deserve this?

"You don't have to deserve anything. Just accept it.

It's my happiness you are sensing."

He tried to answer in kind. The truth of his love and desire for her love communicated clearly. Confusion was there also, but with less ferocity.

He began to relax as they strolled along the water's edge, carrying their shoes so they could wade in the lapping waves.

She laughed happily. "We may actually enjoy being together—even have fun!" She giggled as they high stepped over fast coming waves the tide was bringing in.

Noah romped through the water with her. He let the retreating waves take the rest of his tension out to sea.

CHAPTER 33

Jake had joined the Circle at their invitation. His tenor blended well in the 'singing.' It was clear to all that the Circle accepted his male energy.

At the end of the ceremony, he and Misha asked to talk with the group. Jake had invited Noah also to please join them.

That he and Misha were together was well known by everyone. No announcement was needed. However, they asked if they might have a joining ceremony here within the Circle; that is, would it be acceptable to the others?

The group's response was a unanimous, "Yes! When?"

Noah surprised everyone: "What do you think about combining a celebration for the completion of the structure with your nuptial? It would be a way to include everyone within an expanded Circle."

Everyone was delighted. Expansion, at last, was taking place.

It was left to Gemma to let the admin group know of the proposed plan. With their blessing, preparations began. She suggested that representatives from each of the volunteer groups be included in the planning. This would make it clear to everyone that this was a community celebration, not just a private party for the Circle (as everyone now called it).

Everyone was excited about the 'joining ceremony' (as it came to be called) for Jake and Misha. Each group wanted to do some kind of presentation at the celebration as their gift to the couple. The energy unleashed by all these preparations was palpable to everyone.

* * *

While Noah worked tirelessly to help complete finishing touches on the structure and offering his help to the individual groups whenever he was asked, there were still empty spaces in his life. He had not joined the

Circle. Nor had he and Brit talked about a future together. What was going to happen after the celebration?

Noah knew Brit felt his anguish. But somehow he couldn't believe he could have her unless he joined the Circle. He Knew his ambivalence came from his experience in the past with The Elders. Their betrayal of the Gatherers infuriated him still. It made trust in something as vague as a Circle seem impossible.

Yet, he had seen nothing negative from the growing group participation in the Circle. They emerged happier, more energetic, and hopeful. He did not think they could Hear the messages, however. Why not?

Was this Shift really different from what the Elders were sure it would be? Opening to Brit was one thing— she was unique. He wasn't so ready to trust the others... Except for Jake and Misha.

Working kept him involved with the other volunteers who worked on the structure. But it didn't keep his nagging thoughts at bay.

What *did* he want? That was easy—he wanted Brit. Where could they find a good life together? A visual image of the dome filled his mind... And his heart yearned for the vision of happy people creating gardens, inventing ways to preserve and transport food to the other Circles... *Circles*? He gasped at what was being revealed—and Brit: so happy in that environment —and with him! No manipulation came from her—to force him to join the Circle. She offered an open invitation, nothing more. And he was going to accept it —on his terms. He smiled to himself as he remembered their night together. After all, she had accepted him.

He released the vision, then swallowed, and finally quieted his accelerated breathing. He pushed back impending tears. What was happening to him? He shook his head. Why had he been fighting everything he wanted?

* * *

Lilla's sparkle, when she returned from her choral rehearsals, made everyone happy. She was discovering not only that she had a lovely singing voice, but that she was happy bonding with others. Her vision of the future became clearer as she worked with everyone to create a special presentation, not just for her sisters, but for the community. It led to thoughts of creating a community at home.

She realized that 'home' meant North, with her boys

—and maybe someday their wives, even grandchildren. She would have so much to share.

Risa Knew her home was waiting for her. Refugees needed more than food and a respite from travel. They could build a community right there! It would give everyone who came to them a dream, hope for themselves and their children.

Her urgency pushed her to enlist other riders to put on an equestrian demonstration for the celebration. It might open their eyes to see how The Shift has awakened even the animals.

She wondered whether she could let the horses demonstrate on their own? She would ask her mare, Sunshine—and maybe Diablo.

Gemma had the gift of falling asleep almost as soon as her head reached her pillow. If she dreamed, she didn't remember. She was up before anyone else and was accused of being chirpy.

So, the one morning she slept in, both Brit and Misha made a couple of comments.

"I dreamed," Gem said. "But... I never dream," she insisted, more to herself than to them.

Brit and Misha glanced at one another before turning their full attention to Gem, waiting to see if she would share.

Gem look puzzled, even uncertain.

Brit encouraged her, "Maybe telling us about it will help."

Gemma hesitated, but then said, "I saw Terri."

Misha looked questioning at Brit, who shook her head slightly. "I don't think I know a Terri," Brit said.

"No. No, you wouldn't." Gem took a deep breath before she continued. "Many years ago, we were a couple. She left me when I joined The Gathering. Her reaction to it wasn't exactly positive!" Gem rubbed her head vigorously as if trying to erase the image or the memory.

"And you haven't seen her or heard from her since?"

"No." It was apparent to both Brit and Misha that she was upset.

Misha shyly asked, "Where did you see her—in your dream, I mean?"

"In my home—North! A bottle-blond still wearing that stetson and that awful, gaudy belt buckle."

"Why do you think she was there?" asked Brit, trying not to smile.

Misha interjected, "How did you feel about her being

there in your home?"

"My heart hurt," Gem said. Then she shook herself and said, "Hey, it was just a dream!"

"Yes, but you don't dream," said Brit. She waited for Gem's response, but there was none.

"Well, I hope that doesn't happen too often— dreaming, I mean—I'm late to the Adminers!" Gemma tried to laugh it off, but she wasn't successful in hiding her feelings.

Brit spoke to Misha after Gem had hurriedly dressed and left. "I think we have to let her sort this out herself."

"But this person is probably waiting for her," Misha insisted.

"Maybe. It sure seems we are all being nudged to get going," Brit quipped. As she gathered her kit for work, she said, "Not much happening at the med center these days." She smiled at Misha. "So, if you want to hang out with Jake—"

Misha grinned. "If you think that's OK."

"Go! Go! Enjoy. Be happy!" As Brit watched her go, she thought to herself how wonderful it was to see Misha so happy.

As Brit left for the medical unit, she softly giggled, relishing her own happiness.

Remembering…

Brit had welcomed Noah. "So, you are coming?" she asked.

He nodded and embraced Brit. "Yes. I definitely am coming with you—with all of us." He took a step back and looked deeply into her eyes, "However, I think my mission is somewhat different from yours."

Brit wanted to protest but kept her mouth firmly closed. "Not separate," he added. "I need you beside me —as my wife." He held her tightly before releasing her. "You'll see!" He gave her a light kiss on her lips and quickly left, with a new bounce in his step.

Brit watched him leave, her mouth opening to demand he come back and explain himself—then closing it as she became aware that her tumbling emotions were definitely inhibiting any Knowing. That calmed her down. Trust. That was her issue, her challenge right now.

The important thing is that Noah wants to come with me *North!* How different it will be this time.

CHAPTER 34

The rumbles were unsettling. They had begun again, after being quiet for the last few months. Were they the last aftershocks from the Big One, or were they the beginnings of the next?

Noah and Jake teamed up to inspect and assign crews where needed or when a discovered weakness indicated repair or reinforcement was required. The planners also decided that the festivities for the Celebrations should be held outside—just in case.

At the same time, preparations were being made for the group's departure. Risa talked to Noah, asking him to train with Misha's horse before embarking on their journey. They rode together each morning, to acquaint him with Risa's training techniques. The intuitive horse guided him through its paces, making their introduction pleasurable. Noah wasn't new to riding, but he was impressed with the ease of communication with Cloud.

These mornings also allowed Risa and Noah an opportunity to clear the air between them. They both acknowledged the awkwardness each felt. Risa was the first to bring up the past, apologizing for her behavior. She said she had hoped for a relationship with him and admitted she had used the lure of her ranch to interest him. "Yes, it was very manipulative—and naïve. You only had eyes for Brit."

Embarrassed, Noah owned his part. "After all, I accepted your invitation to visit. It wasn't just the ranch I was interested in," he said with a smile at her. "I admit I was tempted by both you and the ranch."

Risa was pleasantly surprised that he would admit it. She also Knew that he was sincere.

As they grew more comfortable with each other, she answered his questions about the women's journey to LA.

"Actually, how dangerous was the trip?" he asked. "Brit has told me very little."

Risa described how they had repulsed marauders with the power of their voices.

He was intrigued and asked for a demonstration. She laughed out loud but declined to demonstrate. How in the world could she duplicate the extraordinary, piercing howl that had erupted simultaneously from each voice, growing to an inhuman screech that sent the intruders running for their lives?

Noah Heard enough of her memory to be staggered.

"It came from us. We didn't do anything to make it happen. Anyway, word traveled fast through the mountain pass. People had heard the 'howl of the banshees' from a group of women traveling toward the sea. We had no more trouble.

"That is when I accepted The Shift and its awesome power. I Knew it would protect our mission to serve. We didn't know what that meant at the time. I mean, we don't see into the future—well, maybe Misha does sometimes."

They exchanged a smile.

She was quiet as she thought about that time. She Knew Noah was looking for answers about their Circle, and how The Shift was part of it.

"How was The Shift part of it? I can't help you with that," she said, responding to his unspoken question. "All I know is that—at least for me—it didn't happen all at once." After a few paces, she went on, "I think it began even before the Big One; I just wasn't aware. My horses, especially Sunshine, seemed to intuit my wishes before they even became conscious." She laughed again. "I thought it was just my amazing skill!"

Noah smiled with her as he remembered his own journey to LA. Things he couldn't explain—how his needs were met or people showing up to help just when he could have been in trouble. He grinned as he remembered how he kept saying to himself, 'Boy, am I lucky!' He began to share this with Risa, and then realized she would Know, but only because his energy had opened to her.

She laughed once more. "Yeah, that's how it starts!" she said as she signaled Sunshine to a canter.

* * *

The rumblings were increasing, putting everyone on edge.

Gemma drew Jake and Misha aside, "Since the two of you are staying after your ceremony, what do you think about forming a new Circle here—with all the new participants?"

Jake and Misha looked at each other, mulling over the implications of forming a new Circle. All the women as well as Jake had been bombarded with questions about their Circle, their 'singing-without-words,' as well as the energy that radiated around the group, shielding them from fear of another Mega-quake.

Misha and Jake were aware of the dangers of being the center of a group of new participants. These new people would need to experience the power within themselves, not look to Misha or Jake for answers to their problems or even to their questions. Misha had shared with Jake how difficult it had been in the beginning for each of the women to accept that the energy generated by the Circle actually came from each of them as they became united in their Intent.

Could Misha and Jake help them attain that inner power? Would they be open to The Shift?

Gem argued that when the group departed for the North, those left behind might feel abandoned. Misha understood immediately and agreed. Jake had to think it through first, but he came to the same conclusion.

When Gem broached the plan, first to Brit and Lilla, they tuned in immediately.

Risa Heard as she was heading toward the enclave. She waited for Noah to catch up to her, and then explained to him the new plan—aloud, to be sure he understood the implications. Everyone agreed it was time for Misha and Jake to take the lead.

"Yes," Noah said, "It's time to move into the next phase." He then silently urged his horse home.

CHAPTER 35

The duo-celebration preparations were progressing rapidly in spite of the rumblings. Infectious laughter broke out sporadically throughout the compound. Smiles were common among the workers.

At the supply centers, when the compound's food crews arrived to restock, they were bombarded with questions. People working throughout the broken city were intensely curious. Rumors had spread about strange women who sang at their compound. How come the volunteers who worked long hours were so happy that they wanted to celebrate? What was there to celebrate?

When the crew described how fast the structure was being erected, or how nice the women were, and that there was about to be a wedding, they were met with extreme skepticism. How did their structure get built so quickly? What kind of wedding? Who was getting married? And what about the 'strange' women who did weird singing?

When the crew leaders reported to Noah and Jake about the reception they were getting, the men conferred with the sisters.

"Let's invite them to the celebration!" was Gemma's first response.

The others enthusiastically agreed. Jake suggested that he and Noah accompany the food crews to the supply centers and deliver their invitation to both celebrations in person.

It wasn't difficult for the men to get a fast acceptance. People wanted to see for themselves what was so special. Noah asked, "Would anyone like to come and help with the preparations?"

The strangers expressed surprise at the invitation, but Noah could see their suspicion lessen. One or two of the men said they would like to come and see for themselves what was going on.

Jake assured them they would be most welcome.

Little by little, visitors started coming to the enclave and were invited to sit in on the admin group meetings or help out with one of the teams. Jake hoped that they would take back ideas and tips to their own groups. If they asked, a volunteer would go back with them to help train their volunteers.

Gemma spoke with Jake and Misha. Would they consider visiting outside groups? Misha was very enthusiastic about this kind of outreach. Jake wanted to take on the challenge as well. But he wanted the two of them to listen first to what other communities were hoping to learn or achieve. Once their intent was clear, he and Misha could focus their energy on supporting them.

The question the sisters did not have an answer for was, should they introduce the concept of The Shift? Perhaps the visitors would discover it themselves when it surfaced in their lives.

Misha said, "Surely, the Circle will provide the answer."

The others murmured their hope.

The community was excited that Jake and Misha were being invited by outsiders to help. The sisters had been uncertain about how outreach would take place. Clearly, modeling was the answer to opening doors.

This led them to consider establishing centers in the North. They could become models within their own communities. Their dreams crystallized in their evening Circles.

As the Circle expanded, the newer participants were asking, "Who is the leader? Are there rules? How could they join?"

It was imperative to the sisters that they make clear there were no leaders. Everyone was a leader. They demonstrated the principle by asking a different participant each evening to begin the hum and carry it into the song-without-words.

Most found the idea uniquely difficult: "Don't we need instruction? How will we know how to do it right?"

The sisters chose not to answer. They just invited the questioners to blend in with their own voices.

At times a participant would attempt to convey a message. In the beginning, there were many requests for help from some deity or other, or complaints about others. The sisters mentored each one, hoping to redirect the requests into determinations to find solutions. Complaints were basically ignored unless they became habitual.

When a message was authentic, the group would accept the intent spoken. If bogus, such as an egoistic attempt to exert some control over the group, Jake would approach that person, inviting them to leave the Circle. The new participants learned.

The work was intense but joyful for the sisters. They were learning patience, seeing how important it was for the new participants to experience the Circle, step by step, as they had.

'Allowing' a message to emerge rather than attempting to 'create' one was perhaps the most difficult to learn. The sisters held the inner space for it to happen for each one.

CHAPTER 36

Noah wasn't yet ready to join the Circle. Instead, he found himself hanging out with the people who were gathered around the fringes of the Circle each evening. They listened but did not participate.

He started asking some of them: "What are you looking for? What keeps you coming back?" Noah wanted to know what they thought about faith. Did they have a faith—in anything? If so, faith in what?

Of course, he was asking himself the same questions. And his answers were not that different from what he heard from others. To some, the Circle was very special but seemed too exclusive. There appeared to be a hierarchy, although Noah knew that was not their intent. For Noah, the vision to create many Circles suggested an equality among participants.

In the early days, as the earthquakes kept coming

after the first Big One, he had heard many stories from disillusioned, numb, or angry people fed up with faith in anything. But when people came and found work on the structure, salvaging whatever was left, he saw hope begin to emerge. With the arrival of the sisters (as he had started to call them), their Circle had galvanized the volunteer workers into actual optimism.

But even that concerned him. Would people be able to withstand the temptation to make the sisters into a version of the Elders, which he despised? Would some kind of oversight be possible, or would that just invite another layer of authority?

So far, Noah observed only positive aspects of the Circle. But he was still perturbed by people's worries:

"I'm not about to give my power away," was one declaration.

When he asked what they meant by power, their answer was, "To think for myself; the ability to make independent decisions."

What Noah heard was their fear of another heartbreaking disillusionment.

How had Brit overcome that, he asked himself? She had been subjected to the charismatic lure of someone who only wanted power for himself. She was crushed as the evidence revealed that the Elders were charlatans

—out for their own benefit—or worse—power over others.

Could The Shift prevent this kind of self-deception? Hopefully. But for those looking for a guru or some super thing i.e., the Circle, to save them from taking responsibility for themselves, he wasn't so sure. Could they bypass the power of The Shift? Ignore it? Deny it? Or even turn against the Circle—declaring it evil, or the sisters, a coven of witches?

Noah shook his head, stood up, and stamped his feet in his frustration with human nature and all the ways they had developed to cope with frightening or just unpleasant aspects of life. He certainly didn't have all the answers—way above his pay grade, he smirked.

But maybe he *could help*: be a bridge, a communication link that could unite those with similar goals. *That* he was sure Brit would understand—and he would also be able to protect her.

He was determined to work things out in his own way and time, and hopefully, be able to help others as he did.

* * *

The special day was coming up fast. The sequence of events had been set in motion by the event planners. Misha had asked for a Circle at sunrise. She and Jake both requested a buffet breakfast be provided for the whole community following their ceremony.

Early afternoon would be the volunteer and crew presentations, ending with Lilla's singers' performance. The day would end with dancing on the sand, accompanied by guitars and wooden flutes.

The group going North would be leaving the next day. All preparations had been made. They were ready.

* * *

On the celebration morning, Brit was relieved to find Noah in bed beside her. "Get up! Lazybones," she roused him, reminding him that the DAY had arrived. Even before dawn, they could see that the sky was crystal clear. They hurriedly dressed and went out to join the gathering crowd.

Everyone was intensely curious about what this first 'joining' ceremony in their community would be like. In the predawn chill, the chatter was light-hearted, excited. A few were checking out the small stage made out of risers. They supposed that would be for each group's presentation.

Brit hurried away to join Misha and the sisters who were getting the bride ready for her nuptial ceremony. Noah had gone to find Jake. The shape of the ceremony had presented itself to them in their Circle the evening before.

A private space was designated a short distance from the small stage to accommodate the couple and the sisters. An outer circle was prepared for the people attending.

Women had offered the sisters some of their cherished, saved material to fashion into the wedding gown Brit and Gemma then designed. Gem and Brit gathered thin strands of flower-like seaweed they could attach to the long Grecian styled tunic that Misha would wear, which included a headband for her hair. Risa and Lilla assigned themselves the task of collecting long strands of kelp to line a path from the ocean to the Circle. Everyone wanted to play a part in this special day.

* * *

Noah found Jake pacing in a small circle, trying to remember the exact words he was to speak. He looked up in gratitude when Noah showed up.

"Do I look OK?"

"Well, since a tuxedo isn't readily available..." Noah gave Jake a big grin. "I guess you'll do."

Jake had found among his friends someone who had saved a white, 60s type shirt—very romantic looking, and who was willing to loan it to him for this momentous occasion.

"Thanks, you are a big help. Noah, look at this and tell me what you think." Jake extricated from his pocket a pale, green ring twined out of a reed he'd discovered along the shore.

Noah took it in his hand. "It's so delicate—and beautiful," he said. Turning it over, he added, "Strong. Like Misha. It's perfect."

"OK, then." Jake took in a deep breath and let it go in a huge sigh. "Let's make this happen!"

Noah laughed with him, clapping him on his shoulder as they started toward the ceremonial Circle.

Noah ushered the people attending to the outer circle where they would watch. Once the rustling and whispered exchanges had ceased, it became quiet. Jake stood among the crowd that faced the ocean. Everyone was turned toward the kelp-lined path, eager to see the bride appear.

The melodic hum from the sisters reached the listeners first, then they saw the four sisters walking slowly, side by side along the path. As they approached, they parted to form the inner Circle.

Jake moved forward two steps to better see the vision of Misha approaching—it was as if she were a goddess emerging from the ocean. Her long silvery hair lit by the rising sun was only bound by the woven hairband around her forehead; her long Grecian tunic was decorated by the flowers from the sea. Her feet were bare in the sand. Her aura became visible to everyone as she stepped up to the edge of the Circle.

People watching were awed as they saw emanating from the center of the Circle, a glow of light that seemed to beckon the couple toward the center of the Circle. Misha began walking toward the center as Jake joined her from the other side. As the hum became the song-without-words, the glow became a swirling, undulating blue-green light that encircled the couple, then the sisters, and expanded to include all those watching. And then there was a hush.

As One, the sisters began a choral chanting:

"Come—Come—Combine your energies—your hearts and your minds."

Misha and Jake, as one chanted their response: "Our intent—to become—as One."

Chorus: "Each so different. Gifts to share."

Misha: "Joy in the life renewed by the other."

Jake: "Dreams coming true, always together."

Chorus: "Storms will come."

Misha and Jake: "And then disburse."

Chorus: "Strength and Confidence."

Misha and Jake: "Giving Hope to all Others."

As the ribbons of light continued to flow about them, Jake retrieved the ring from his pocket, and gently placed it on Misha's ring finger. Their kiss was greeted with oohs and aahs from all attending and then exploded into delighted applause as tiny particles of light, caught by the sun, began drifting down like confetti over participants and guests.

As the couple left the Circle hand in hand, Gemma stepped forward to address the crowd: "Everyone!

Please join us to share in the Breakfast Buffet that has been prepared by the Community."

Of all the special events prepared by the community groups that afternoon, it was the equine demonstration that fascinated the crowd. There were no riders or instructors, just horses doing their thing.

The horses displayed intricate patterns, moving individually, sometimes together to create a dance of horses. No one had ever witnessed such a display.

The skits, along with proclamations to rebuild and reclaim the great City of Los Angeles, were warmly received. The original songs and guitar duets were enthusiastically applauded.

The final presentation was in two parts. Lilla and two colleagues had formed a trio and sang the famous trio of 'Three Little Maids from School...' from Gilbert and Sullivan's "Mikado." This was followed by the chorus singing a medley of Broadway love songs. Each member had selected a favorite song, which was then combined into a medley that the chorus performed. Misha thought it was all quite wonderful, and Jake basked in her happiness.

The dancing might have been mainly a shuffle in the sand, but it provided an opportunity for everyone to come together in a joyful expression of their caring community.

Noah had shown Jake his and Brit's special cove, which the couple then had made very special for Misha's and Jake's night together.

CHAPTER 37

The Community turned out the next day to send the travelers off with good wishes and expressions of appreciation. Noah, riding Cloud, and Brit with Diablo led the group along the shoreline. The sisters were a little sad, as well as a little glad they were heading home. They felt that they had done well and fulfilled their mission here. What new ones were ahead?

This group of travelers was a larger contingent than had come from the North. Among them, there were five horse handlers with their mounts who wanted to join Risa at her ranch. She welcomed them warmly.

Lilla and her new friends, Sally and Jane, had become very close as they rehearsed for the festivities. When it was over, they asked Lilla if they could stick with her—maybe do singing on the trail. Lilla was delighted, knowing that Sally came with her guitar.

Everyone would look forward to sing-a-longs in the evenings. And as she considered how her boys would welcome young female company, Lilla needed no persuasion.

Professor Gary Zonger, a botanist who had worked at UCLA before the Big One hit, had gotten to know Noah and Brit. The more he heard about Noah's greenhouse dome experiments, the more he wanted to join them. They were more than happy to include him.

Gemma had invited along a young couple who just wanted a new start in a new place. She had let them know her 'digs' were pretty basic, but they were welcome to stake out an area close by for their own.

* * *

In the morning, before the caravan departed, Misha asked that they gather together one more time. Her words were directed especially to the new people who had joined the sisters.

"The strength of our connection is dependent on the inner development of each one of us. Negativity from even one participant can create a glitch in our ability to communicate with each other in North Valley as well as with those here in Los Angeles."

The travelers signaled their understanding. They felt how essential it was they maintain a constant connection. As one, they reaffirmed that they would maintain their bonds.

As the large group got underway, Misha and Jake stood and watched as little by little the caravan faded from sight. Jake held Misha close as her tears streamed. She would miss her sisters.

* * *

The group traveled slowly at first as everyone got used to moving together. Eventually, they adjusted to the pace as well as to the many tasks involved in setting up camp and then breaking it down.

Everyone was invited to join the evening Circle Ceremony. Most of the newcomers were eager to participate. Their experience in observing the nuptial ceremony had awed and intrigued them. They hoped to feel the energy of the Circle for themselves. They were not disappointed.

Noah participated in the Circle but maintained his dedication to finding common ground with people of any belief or faith as long as they held the same Intent: to Serve others. Evenings around the campfire, after all the singing, encouraged conversation, and some of the group sought him out with their questions.

Living close to the women and with each other enabled the new participants to be easily integrated into the Circle of Intent.

The size of the group and the fact they were traveling with several men this time, discouraged any outside interference as they traveled through the mountain passes.

The Circle they formed each evening felt small, and at first, their hum seemed thin. But, as the new participants gained experience, it gradually increased and swelled into the song-without-words. When the sound faded away, each was beginning to experience Listening and Feeling their energies merge and gather strength—becoming a message: "all is well."

Once through the mountains, following their evening ritual, and before the group began preparing for travel across the desert, Risa announced: "Sunshine and Diablo are expecting a foal in the spring! I sense that two of the other horses are expecting as well."

Risa let the group know she had confided to Misha and Jake her intention to return to the compound two out of every three horses born on her ranch. New hope permeated the entire group as they grasped the significance of new life.

Their mission in LA was complete, and for the most part, there was a relaxed atmosphere among both the seasoned and the inexperienced travelers.

They passed uneventfully through the mountain passes. Weather issues, which had bedeviled the sisters' journey to LA, were absent as they began their trek across the desert.

When they arrived at the familiar oasis at the edge of the desert just as sunset fell, Noah announced it was a good place to have a powwow. No one disagreed.

He encouraged the weary riders to stretch their legs, relax, and enjoy a leisurely meal for a change. The sisters knew that the smaller mountain range ahead awaited, but the united group had developed the confidence needed to complete their journey successfully.

"We have decisions to make," Gemma began. "We will soon be at the fork in the road. We need to let everyone know the main group will be splitting up and going in different directions."

They had become very attuned to one another, and as a result, there were growing concerns about how each group on their own would fare. Everyone agreed that communication between all the groups was vital. Did they have to have a format for messages between them? Was a representative needed from each group? It was clear there was much to discuss… and to learn about how to harness The Shift that would make their communication possible.

But beyond their concerns, it was clear they had bonded, and they could communicate with each other—and with their friends still in Los Angeles.

Risa spoke, "Wouldn't it be wise if we all stop at the ranch? It will give everyone a chance to rest and prepare for being on their own."

Brit let Noah know that their electric car was still at Risa's. This brought a broad grin to his face.

"I certainly wouldn't mind a hot shower before going on," he said.

They all laughed their agreement.

When the newcomers were told that they were planning to stop and refresh at Risa's ranch, there was growing anticipation. The travelers were curious as well as relieved that they would get a respite from their journey.

Within a short time, they reached the open valley that stretched ahead.

As their caravan got a first glimpse of the ranch, Lilla was the first to voice their surprise, "So many more people." They all could see the many small dwellings that dotted the land beyond the ranch house.

Risa searched the landscape and finally spotted Carlos, mounted on his sturdy horse, riding to greet them. As he got closer, she slid off Sunshine and ran to meet him. He dismounted and welcomed her with a warm embrace. He then addressed the group, "Welcome to Ms. Risa's ranch. We have a banquet prepared for you."

When they finally reached the ranch house, youngsters ran happily to each rider, taking the reins of the horses as the riders dismounted and followed Carlos and Risa. Risa suggested everyone go into the house and freshen up.

Once everyone had again gathered, Carlos led them to the tables situated under a canopy erected in front of the ranch house. Before the travelers were platters of fruit, fresh raw vegetables, and slices of ham on freshly baked bread. Pitchers of iced tea looked especially inviting to the thirsty group.

Everyone murmured their appreciation to Carlos for his warm welcome, and then quickly sat at Risa's invitation to please relax and enjoy.

The two men and three women who would be staying at the ranch with Risa were somewhat overwhelmed. The ranch seemed a small community. As they walked to join the others, they asked among themselves, "Who is this handsome Latino, Carlos? Does he run the place? Is he going to be our new boss?"

In the meantime, Carlos asked to speak with Risa in the main room. She was anxious to be brought up to speed on what was happening here at the ranch. She also intended to ask him about the 'messages' she had received.

As they sat together at the long table, close but not touching, Risa attempted to put aside her excitement at being with Carlos.

He was not blind to the electric energy between them. He smiled at her, and a deep calm came over her. She breathed deeply and then quieted. She could return his smile.

He began, "Refugees from both LA and from further North have been finding their way here to the ranch. I need your thoughts and your permission on how best to accommodate these people. I believe it is only the beginning."

She Heard his concern and deep feelings for the refugees.

"I feel we must provide shelter, and even more important, rules of behavior." He looked for her response. "But if it is not the vision you have for the ranch—I see the many people you have brought with you—I am ready to lead my people and any of the refugees who wish to join us, to a different place."

"Please!" She reached out her hand, placing it firmly on his arm. "Do not even consider leaving." Somewhat shaken, she said, "Our goal—my goal is to serve. What better place than here?"

He put his own hand over hers. "I felt this was true, but I needed to be sure. I will begin—" then quickly added, "if you wish."

She nodded her acceptance. "We will work together."

Carlos looked deeply into her eyes, sighed happily. "Of course." He left the table for the exit.

Risa remained sitting, wondering at the speed this was progressing. Carlos seemed to have taken his calming effect with him. She was jittery with excitement.

* * *

Gemma told Brit and Noah that she would be leaving with Lucy and Lucky—the couple who had joined her —in the morning. She was anxious to be home.

Brit gave her a knowing look as she said, "Of course. We understand. Tonight let's get Lilla and Risa and make a communication plan. We need to be sure we stay in contact."

As Gemma left to make arrangements and then talk to Risa, Brit said to Noah, "Lucy and Lucky? That can't be their real names."

He laughed. "Like you've said, it's all about new beginnings."

Lilla was pleased to be walking, not riding, as she showed Sally and Jane around the ranch. They quickly met up with three other musicians from Carlos' group, who caught sight of Sally's guitar and invited them to come play. They made a plan to perform tonight as part of a celebration welcome.

Jane let them know they were also a trio and would love to sing as well. That was enthusiastically accepted.

While Lilla was eager to be home once again with her sons, this night sounded like such fun—packing and preparations could wait one more day.

Brit and Noah retired to their assigned room. They took one look at the double bed and reached for each other.

That night there was music, guitars, flutes along with homemade tambourines, and much singing. Wine made from local grapes flowed. Dancing—a performance, and then an invitation for everyone to join in. It was a joyful celebration of new beginnings.

* * *

All the Circles agreed to communicate together once a week at the same time. An agenda was not needed unless one group requested time. They discussed whether that was often enough, and what they should do if there were an emergency.

Gem suggested, "We can train the newcomers to Listen once a day at a certain time of day for any message coming through. It will serve the dual purpose of training the new people as well as staying connected.

Once settled, they all helped Gem get her essentials put aside for the next day's departure. Risa gave her blessing to take the Ginger and the other two horses. "My gift," she said, giving Gemma a farewell hug.

Lucy and Lucky were a little reluctant to leave the ranch's warmth and safety quite so soon. However, they went along when Gem told them about the communication training and a plan for a Big Celebration with everyone once a year. All the Circles would come together for a full week of feasting and being together. These happy thoughts helped overcome their resistance to once again, having to mount their horses.

"On horseback, it will only take us a few hours to get to my cabin," Gem said to them. "I am so grateful I don't have to walk!" she said and then described the full day it had taken her to walk to Brit's dome.

Gem had warned the couple that they would need to use their tent until a structure was built. They had no issue with that. By now, they Knew Gem, and they were excited to have an opportunity to begin their new life there.

Terri had Heard that Gem was on her way home. She was nervous and excited at the same time. To wick off all her extra energy, she had done the unthinkable for her: she cleaned the cabin from top to bottom, washing as best she could all the curtains, and after a lovely rain, she opened up all the windows to bring in to the small cabin the gloriously fresh air.

It was a small, rustic, but comfortable place. Only one bedroom, which she fervently hoped wouldn't be a problem. She ran her fingers through her cropped, blond hair. *Well, I'll solve that problem if it comes up.*

Once Gem and her companions could smell the smoke coming from a chimney off in the distance, all signs of fatigue from Lucy and Lucky faded away.

For Gem, when she saw Terri standing there on her porch, waving them in, it was the promise of a welcome home. Gem urged her horse to a faster pace. Knowing that Terri would soon be in her arms, took Gemma's breath away. Tears coursed down her cheeks. She couldn't remember feeling a love so intensely. Finally arriving, she slid from her horse and ran to embrace Terri.

Lucy, watching this 'homecoming,' looked at Lucky, who raised his eyebrows and gave a nod to Lucy. They turned to leave, just as Gem turned back, and called to them:

"You don't have to leave. I was just so surprised—happily," she said, looking at Terri.

Terri echoed the invitation, "Come in—" She waved them to her. "Dinner awaits us!"

No further invitation was needed as plates and bowls appeared on the table. Terri ladled the thick soup into bowls as Lucy, at Terri's direction, brought the freshly baked bread to the table along with plates of butter and blackberry jam.

Lucy gestured to Lucky as she said, "We will clear and wash the dishes."

Gemma smiled her appreciation as she took Terri's arm and guided her outside. "Tell me. Why did you come? Why are you here?"

"Always the straight arrow! I know I debunked the whole Gathering scam—"

Gem's facial expression stopped her.

"Sorry! That's what I thought then."

Gem's voice was tight as she said, "What I am about

now has nothing to do with that group."

Terri reached out to her, "Gem, I know that. I Know
—I Heard! I can't explain—"

Gem interrupted, "None of us can, but we call it The
Shift."

"Ah—OK. Great. At least I can name it." She gave a
short laugh—and then a tender look at Gem, and said,
"I never wanted to leave you. I just couldn't stomach
that crew you all called 'The Elders.'"

Gem shrugged, then admitted, refusing to look at
Terri, "You were right. I hate to admit that."

"I know—believe me, I know," she said with a smirk.

Gem gave an exaggerated huff.

Terri just laughed in amusement. "Hey," she said,
putting an arm around Gem, "I'm here because I don't
want to live in this new world without you. I love you
—always have."

Gem let go of her stiff defensiveness as she Heard
Terri. Her own heart opened with a huge appreciation
that Terri had sought her out. She chuckled to herself as
she realized that Terri was part of the 'group,' whether
she Knew it yet or not.

With that thought, she took a deep breath, put her
own arm around Terri, and let her tears flow.

"Hey, Gem! Where do we set up our tent?" yelled

Lucy from the doorway.

Laughing, they all came together to help pitch the tent a short distance from the cabin.

* * *

The following day, Lilla, Sally, and Jane left on their horses, gifted by Risa.

When Lilla and the two girls arrived home, no one was around. Where were the boys?

It didn't feel deserted. The house was in good order. Just empty. She was somewhat disappointed, but she didn't feel that anything was wrong. She was gratified that the boys had made so much progress in restoring the cabin.

She showed Sally and Jane the minimal quarters and then set about checking cupboards for supplies. She found tea and put the kettle on the wood-stove that was still warm.

The door abruptly swung open, and two young men came in.

"Oh my gosh! You're men!" Lilla yelled and ran to hug her two surprised sons.

"Hi, Mom! We thought we'd get back before you got

here."

"You Knew I was coming?" She just looked at them with an open mouth.

"Well, yeah—you practically yelled at us days ago," laughed her eldest, Tomas.

Ricardo shyly said, "Glad you're back, Mom."

Lilla's eyes filled, then she turned and indicated Sally and Jane, "Meet two friends." She laughed at their expressions and then said, "We are all going to create music!" Lilla just laughed again at their bewildered faces.

Finally, Ricardo grinned. "Hey, can we have food first? Come on, Tomas. Let's bring in the groceries," he said as he stopped ogling Sally, the very pretty brunette.

Tomas seemed captivated by Jane's copper curls. She was looking back at him with great interest. She asked, "Can I help?"

"Absolutely!" Tomas said and gallantly ushered her through the open door.

After Lilla and the four young people had eaten their fill, Lilla told them about her journey and the Circle ceremony they would initiate the next day.

The boys had no difficulty understanding The Shift.

They had been bombarded with Lilla's messages ever since she had left. Sally and Jane joined in with stories of their own, describing life at the compound and the extraordinary wedding and the celebration they had witnessed just before they left. Finally, admitting their exhaustion, everyone found a bed.

Lilla reached out to her sisters, sending a virtual message that the Circle ceremony would begin the following evening. The reply came quickly: 'Glad you are safely home.' With that assurance, she went to bed happy that she truly was home—and slept.

* * *

Brit and Noah, and their new friend, Gary, had the luxury of driving their electric car, fully charged, back to their dome house. Diablo and Cloud would remain at the ranch.

Noah was especially eager to get home. He wanted to know how well his emergency measures had held up.

Brit's enthusiasm about the dome, especially how safe she felt even during all the quakes, deeply moved him. Their relationship had become a true partnership. That he had been able at last to ignite her passion, which he so needed from her, was extremely fulfilling. He felt that her full acceptance of him was without reservations.

Driving the car seemed strange and unbelievably comfortable as well as fast after all those days on horseback. Gary, their botanist friend, asked questions non-stop about the greenhouse dome and what the plans were for developing an outside garden.

Noah kept deflecting the botanist's questions and was especially happy when they pulled up to the dome. It looked exactly as Brit had left it.

Before she could put her key in the lock, Noah stopped her. "Gary, please stand aside for just a moment." He took the key, unlocked, and pushed open the door. And before Brit could rush in, he lifted her into his arms and carried her across the threshold. Before putting her down, he kissed her and whispered in her ear, "To new beginnings."

Gary smiled in appreciation and gathered some of their luggage before coming into the dome behind them.

* * *

Next morning plans were discussed and put into action, thanks to their new colleague, Gary Zonger's expertise and enthusiasm.

Brit wanted to be involved with the house garden as Noah and Gary worked out planting, harvesting, and future distribution of the produce from their mini-farm. As it grew, they would be able to enlist refugees who wanted work.

Along with her greenhouse work, Brit was imagining all the new Circles coming together once a year. Maybe they could call it a festival and invite everyone in the nearby community to come to share in the festivities. Her enthusiasm ebbed slightly as she worried about providing shelter, food—taking care of the waste!

She scaled down her BIG plan to a more modest one, a gathering of her sisters and their new companions.

She was sure they could entice Misha and Jake to come. So much to share!

Gemma would be a treasure with her organizational skills and experience in LA, especially if they extended the gathering to one week.

As she finished her work, she realized this was the night for connecting with the other groups.

At the Circle that evening, she could hardly contain her excitement and insisted she tell everyone her ideas. She was gratified at how receptive everyone seemed.

Later, as he and Brit retired to their room, and started preparing for bed, Noah suggested that he and Gary might have been given a heads up before involving everybody.

"But everyone loved the idea!" she said.

He didn't respond.

She felt the tension developing between them. But before saying anything, she reflected on all the changes in their lives. *Am I expected to consult?* She questioned herself.

She shook her head. *Maybe just share? This is going to take some adjustment.*

She finished getting into her pajamas and approached Noah. She could tell he hadn't quite tuned into the tension she was feeling.

"I need to ask..." She began, then amended, "We both need to share."

"Of course," he readily agreed.

"You expected me to consult with you about my ideas before sharing them with the others. Why?"

Noah's face showed his initial shock at her question.

"Well," he said, "we're a team, yes?"

"So?"

"So, if one of us has an idea or suggestion, doesn't it make sense to share it with us first?"

"For approval?" she questioned.

"Ah—I see where you are at." Noah's voice conveyed his understanding. "Not approval," he said. "Look, an idea shared can be enhanced. Concerns can be worked through. That's what I mean."

Brit exhaled the breath she realized she had been holding. "OK. I Hear you" She looked directly into his eyes as she said, "We've been married, but not really together. It's different for me now."

"For me, too," he confessed. With a smile, he took her hand. "Gary and I need your input, too," he said as he squeezed her hand before letting it go. "The Shift has opened us up, but it seems emotions can shut it down," he observed.

"Yes, that has become very clear," she realized as she said it. "I guess we still have to work to make relationships manageable!"

"I'm game if you are," Noah said.

Brit nodded and then sealed it with a kiss.

CHAPTER 38

Risa felt the absence of her sisters and all their new friends. She decided to throw herself into chores that needed doing. Horses certainly required grooming. Evening would come soon enough, and for the first time, their Circle would be formed at a long distance from each other.

She wanted that connection to work. *Maybe being so dependent on them was not wise. What if...*

Carlos came close to her as she continued grooming Sunshine.

"You are troubled, mi querida."

"Oh—you startled me."

"Lo siento." And he took a step back.

"No, please don't go." He turned back. "Am I troubled? No, not exactly. I think I just miss Lilla's silliness with her new friends—" She resumed her grooming. "I miss the firm confidence that Gemma inspires. And Brit—always ready to fix whatever problem arises." She momentarily stopped her brushing.

"Friends always are with us—here," Carlos said, holding his hand over his heart.

His smile and the soft look in his eyes as he gazed at her warmed her heart.

Risa turned her attention back to Sunshine, and then she shyly asked, "Carlos, are you—and your people—planning to stay?"

"Of course, for as long as you need us."

"And then?" she said, giving her horse long, slow brush strokes.

"What are you asking, Risa?" Carlos studied her as she tried to find the words her heart wanted to say.

"What if—I want you to stay—here, *with* me?" She stopped her brushing and turned to look at him. His arms were opened wide, an invitation she ran into.

He closed his arms around her, and holding her close, he said, "We shall do wonderful things here."

CHAPTER 39

Misha and Jake were delighted with their hidden cove, prepared for them by Brit and Noah. Very little debris was still being thrown onto the shore. A swim together in the ocean was a temptation not to be ignored.

They tasted the salt on their lips as they kissed and were buffeted by gentle waves on their naked bodies, cleansed by the water that had finally become clear. They felt such freedom away from everyone, secure in their secret cove.

Later, as they lay on the warm sand, resting side by side, they talked softly. Jake happily shared his vision with Misha. "I see us traveling North, visiting each of the new Circles in the Valley."

As much as Misha appreciated that The Shift enabled them all to be together in mind, she was excited to know there would be times they would come together, and she could actually hug her sisters.

"Maybe we could all get together in one place once a year—maybe for a whole week—make it a festival," she offered. "We could have it at a different place each year, so hosting all of us wouldn't be too burdensome."

They continued to share their dreams, sometimes simply intertwining their energies, at other times, speaking aloud in warm tones.

After a bit, Jake stood and pulled Misha up beside him. "Come on. One more dip, and then I'll build a fire —and you can make dinner!" he teased.

Misha pushed him away and made a run for the growing waves. He watched her plunge under a large incoming wave and then dove in after her. Dinner could wait.

Afterward, they talked late into the night, talking again about their friends who had left for the North. Everyone would have unique experiences to share, including all that they would learn in LA. Both of them were enthusiastic about their new Circle at the compound—and about supporting those Circles that evolved from there. Their union had become a true partnership. Their work lay before them for years to come.

One question, unspoken, bothered Misha. *Is a family even possible for the two of us with the demands of our mission?*

She began to share this with Jake, but before she completed a sentence, he held her very close. "Our mission will reveal itself. It will always include us—our needs, our wishes. Let's trust in the Circle, and in The Shift within us. All things now are possible."

"But what we do now will determine our future—"

"Exactly." He hugged her closer. "So let's work hard to bring about a world that will welcome and value our children."

CHAPTER 40

ONE YEAR LATER

The festival was underway! After being apart for one year, reunions were emotional and full of laughter. The word, 'gathering' had regained its original meaning—a coming together.

They had agreed that the dome should be the first venue. The logistics of providing shelter, food, and everything needed had been worked out. Brit and Noah were delighted and eager to show their thriving dome greenhouse along with the outdoor plots projected for a mini-farm that could grow with the communities' needs.

Catching up on each one's progress filled the days

and nights. While the groups had been communicating via the Circles, it was still limited to essential messages. A planning committee for developing communication capabilities was to meet during the week.

Lilla's boys had brought brides! Sally and Tomas, Jane and Ricardo proudly showed off the impending arrivals of the next generation. Lilla was over the moon with her new status of grandmother-to-be. She proudly introduced the additional young people who had joined their Circle. Their group infected the rest with their energy and enthusiasm.

All the groups were delighted when Lilla announced that they had brought their musical instruments to provide entertainment each evening. Their creativity and surprising professionalism, thrilled everyone.

Jane explained, "Practicing was our main so-called downtime." Appreciative laughter greeted her explanation.

Risa and Carlos arrived on horses with their many followers. Their happiness and partnership were evident to everyone.

Risa took on the task of rounding up all the

youngsters living at the ranch and from a nearby community to begin instruction on riding and caring for the horses. The children were a little nervous but very excited.

Cloud and her new foal were left at the ranch, but Diablo and Sunshine helped corral all the other horses.

Carlos spent hours with Noah and Gary, learning as much as he could about their farming techniques. When he sensed their openness, Carlos offered his ancestral wisdom about the plants. Noah and Gary were intrigued by the idea to combine his ancient knowledge with their modern technology. It seemed a perfect symbolic path for the future.

His and Risa's goal was to make their ranch self-sufficient. He told them, "This is no small goal with the increasing numbers of refugees who are arriving, many wanting to stay."

Noah was anxious to share with all the groups their most astonishing discovery, thanks to Gary's know-how. They had discovered that aquifers had been driven closer to the surface by the Big Quake. This meant digging wells manually, and that could access water with relatively little hand pumping, should the newly installed solar panels not be adequate.

Noah explained, "Discovering the accessible aquifers

means we are able to expand capacity, but not just at our place. Gary thinks all of you will be able to find water on your property." Everyone became excited about the possibilities. Noah and Gary promised that before everyone went home, they would share the plans they had mapped out for water distribution.

Brit and Noah, along with an exuberant Gary, proudly showed the greenhouse as well as their expanded plans for planting outdoors. Their vision extended to providing fresh produce to the community and eventually establishing a distribution system to connect all the Circle groups.

When asked about the labor involved, Noah shared how they were welcoming the refugees who arrived, looking for food or shelter, or in some cases, a place to put down new roots. Expanding the ranch would enable them to absorb the new, arriving refugees.

Tomas, Lilla's son, asked, "How exactly does that work?"

Noah went into detail. "Everyone is offered an opportunity to work in exchange for food and shelter. Some stay a few days and then move on. Others want to stay and become part of the group. Some have skills and find a natural place here. We offer the less skilled an opportunity to apprentice with one of our people."

Brit, who was watching Tomas' reaction, saw his wheels turning as Noah spoke. She and Lilla exchanged smiles.

Misha and Jake were surrounded with a warm hug and happy welcomes. Everyone was eager to hear about their progress in LA. They enthusiastically shared their news about their growth.

Jake began, "I had no idea how important our last celebrations would be for the expansion of the Circles.

Misha chimed in, "They wanted to get all that energy for themselves!"

"It made it so much easier to present the idea of The Shift, let alone consider the possibility that it is real!" he laughed.

"People loved the idea of singing in a circle," Misha said. "Getting them used to just Listening and then Hearing was not so easy."

Jake interjected, "But it *is happening*." He shrugged sheepishly and added, "Little by little."

Everyone laughed in appreciation.

Later, Misha asked Brit, "What about your Circle?"

Brit said, "Some want to join the Circle, others do

not. All who are in harmony with wanting to serve others, however, are welcomed."

Noah admitted, "Some are solely concerned with their own welfare or how they can benefit. There always will be some who are only takers—no matter the cost to others."

Brit added, "Thanks to The Shift, it's not too difficult to perceive whether a person's tendencies are positive or negative. However, some of them really want to change."

Noah smiled at his wife, and then continued, "To the few who only want a handout, food, and other supplies are given. But we also give them our message: 'We have no room for you here.' Somehow they leave, grateful for the short rest and the gift of provisions."

Noah's peaceful ways of sending away negative forces resonated strongly with Carlos. His own harnessing of positive energies combined with the unity of the Circle was powerful. He envisioned how this would bring Risa and him into even greater harmony.

The last arrivals were Gemma's troop, which were welcomed with enthusiastic embraces, as well as a special welcome as the ladies reached out to Terri, who they had only met through their 'messages.' The surprise was the new arrival expected by Lucy and Lucky, who quickly found and bonded with Lilla's growing family.

Gemma and Terri got to work immediately. Their organizational expertise circumvented glitches that could threaten the festival's success. Their first proposal was to reserve the last days for each group to present their year's experiences, findings, difficulties, and future plans. From the beginning, everyone had agreed that this week should be more than just a reunion.

The shift in emphasis enabled them to make the week a time to share, at times to instruct, and definitely a time to plan for the next year and set goals for the years beyond. All realized that the increasing population throughout the North Valley, not only from the many refugees who continued to arrive but also from the new families emerging, a city could be in the making.

Lilla was determined this reunion should not only be work sessions. "Sally, Jane and I have put together a musical finale for the final night. And we want everyone from the nearby community to be invited. We think they should attend the groups' presentations as well as the final evening's performances."

Sally's plan was to invite the younger children from the community to perform with them. "I'll teach them songs I know they can learn and sing."

Jane added, "I wrote new lyrics to two songs, so they better reflect our new world."

Lilla insisted that the trio once again perform "Three Little Maids from School" song from the 'Mikado' with a few changed lyrics. Finally, they would lead everyone in a sing-along of well-known folk songs.

Gemma, Brit, and Risa clapped enthusiastically when hearing the plans.

The group decided that Jake should give a short explanation of the Circle Ceremony at the end of the performance as well as an introduction to The Shift. He happily agreed.

He was convinced The Shift had been experienced by everyone, whether consciously or not. He hoped his description might awaken more people into a recognition of the positive power within each person.

Then, Risa and Carlos would announce that everyone was invited to their ranch for the next year's reunion—and celebration. They would make a tentative plan and seek Noah's and Brit's hosting experience from this first year.

After a week of shared stories, warm hugs, shared tears, and evolving plans for each of their places, the festival drew to a close. People from the nearby community warmly thanked the sisters and their companions for the wonderful entertainment, and for their services throughout the past year. Their heartfelt thanks and appreciation moved everyone.

Misha then invited everyone to form a Circle. "If you would like, we invite you to join us in our Circle, as we end this most auspicious beginning of our Annual Festival, The Circle of Intent."

Misha and Jake moved to the center of the Circle to begin the hum. As it evolved into the Song-without-words, they moved together, merging with the circle. The song swelled into harmonious tones felt well beyond the Circles into the universes beyond.

As the last sounds faded away, Misha's voice rang out: "Listen. Hear. Know. See. Feel."

Then silence. Each experienced the message within that was meant solely for them.

Finally, each experienced the final message that was voiced by all.

"We are one. As I am—we are. We are The Circle of Intent. We Survive to Serve—as we are, as we can be." Then silence, until Misha's voice invited them to, "SEE!"

As eyes opened, there was a hush of exhaled breath as they experienced the rush of the blue-green light that encircled each person, energetically pulsing throughout the Circle of Intent.

Slowly, the colors and energies faded, and the Circle disbanded wordlessly. People left, flooded emotionally with the experiences of the night. They took with them cherished memories to savor throughout the year.

Until they would meet again.

If you like this story,
would you be so kind as to leave a review?

Reviews are extremely important
to an author's success and greatly appreciated.
Even one sentence helps!

To sign up for Mia's Newsletter,
visit MiaFliers.com

An actress, a teacher, a financial planner, a commissioner, an executive assistant, a librarian—and now, Mia Fliers is an author, who put on paper a life, or lives of people who seek meaning, a purpose for being.

From her childhood Nancy Drew's adventures to the heroines she has portrayed as an actor, Mia Fliers spends her time diving into imaginary worlds. Without fail, she carries a paperback in her bag, whether working or heading to a Nichiren Buddhist meeting.

However, Mia never dreamed that she could write a novel.

A creative writing workshop taught by her friend and former student—awarding-winning playwright, Suzan Zeder —convinced Mia to give it a whirl. "Firecracker: Claire's Journey" and "The Shift" are the results.

Mia fell in love with the process of writing. She is currently working on her third book!